Over the Sliprails by Henry Lawson

Henry Archibald Hertzberg Lawson was born on the 17th June 1867 in a town on the Grenfell goldfields of New South Wales, Australia.

As a youth an ear infection had left him partially deaf and by fourteen he had lost his hearing completely.

He immersed himself in books to make up for the difficulties of a classroom education but later failed to gain entry to a University.

His first published poem was 'A Song of the Republic' in The Bulletin on 1st October 1887. This was quickly followed by other poems with one recognising him as "a youth whose poetic genius here speaks eloquently for itself."

In 1892, The Bulletin engaged him for an inland trip where he could write articles about the harsh realities of life in drought-stricken New South Wales. This resulted in his contributions to the Bulletin Debate and became the experience for a number of his stories in subsequent years. For Lawson this was an eye-opening period. His grim view of the outback was far removed from the romantic idyll of contemporary poetry and literature.

In 1896, Lawson married Bertha Bredt, Jr. but the marriage ended in June 1903. They had two children.

Despite this Lawson was finding his way in the literary world and achieving recognition. His most successful prose collection 'While the Billy Boils', was published in 1896. In it he virtually reinvented Australian realism.

His writing style of short, sharp sentences with honed and sparse descriptions created a personal writing style that defined Australians: dryly laconic, passionately egalitarian and deeply humane.

Sadly, for Lawson despite his growing recognition and fame he became withdrawn and unable to take part in the usual routines of life. His struggles with alcohol and mental health issues continued to drain him. His once prolific literary output began to decline. At times he was destitute mainly due, despite good sales and an enthusiastic audience, to ruinous publishing deals he had entered into.

Henry Archibald Hertzberg Lawson died, of cerebral hemorrhage, in Abbotsford, Sydney on 2nd September 1922.

Index of Contents

The Shanty-Keeper's Wife

There were about a dozen of us jammed into the coach, on the box seat and hanging on to the roof and tailboard as best we could. We were shearers, bagmen, agents, a squatter, a cockatoo, the usual joker—and one or two professional spielers, perhaps. We were tired and stiff and nearly frozen—too cold to talk and too irritable to risk the inevitable argument which an interchange of ideas would have led up to. We had been looking forward for hours, it seemed, to the pub where we were to change horses. For the last hour or two all that our united efforts had been able to get out of the driver was a grunt to the effect that it was "'bout a couple o' miles." Then he said, or grunted, "'Tain't fur now," a couple of times, and refused to commit himself any further; he seemed grumpy about having committed himself that far.

He was one of those men who take everything in dead earnest; who regard any expression of ideas outside their own sphere of life as trivial, or, indeed, if addressed directly to them, as offensive; who, in fact, are darkly suspicious of anything in the shape of a joke or laugh on the part of an outsider in their own particular dust-hole. He seemed to be always thinking, and thinking a lot; when his hands were not both engaged, he would tilt his hat forward and scratch the base of his skull with his little finger, and let his jaw hang. But his intellectual powers were mostly concentrated on a doubtful swingle-tree, a misfitting collar, or that there bay or piebald (on the off or near side) with the sore shoulder.

Casual letters or papers, to be delivered on the road, were matters which troubled him vaguely, but constantly—like the abstract ideas of his passengers.

The joker of our party was a humourist of the dry order, and had been slyly taking rises out of the driver for the last two or three stages. But the driver only brooded. He wasn't the one to tell you straight if you offended him, or if he fancied you offended him, and thus gain your respect, or prevent a misunderstanding which would result in life-long enmity. He might meet you in after years when you had forgotten all about your trespass—if indeed you had ever been conscious of it—and "stoush" you unexpectedly on the ear.

Also you might regard him as your friend, on occasion, and yet he would stand by and hear a perfect stranger tell you the most outrageous lies, to your hurt, and know that the stranger was telling lies, and never put you up to it. It would never enter his head to do so. It wouldn't be any affair of his—only an abstract question.

It grew darker and colder. The rain came as if the frozen south were spitting at your face and neck and hands, and our feet grew as big as camel's, and went dead, and we might as well have stamped the footboards with wooden legs for all the feeling we got into ours. But they were more comfortable that way, for the toes didn't curl up and pain so much, nor did our corns stick out so hard against the leather, and shoot.

We looked out eagerly for some clearing, or fence, or light—some sign of the shanty where we were to change horses—but there was nothing save blackness all round. The long, straight, cleared road was no longer relieved by the ghostly patch of light, far ahead, where the bordering tree-walls came together in perspective and framed the ether. We were down in the bed of the bush.

We pictured a haven of rest with a suspended lamp burning in the frosty air outside and a big log fire in a cosy parlour off the bar, and a long table set for supper. But this is a land of contradictions; wayside shanties turn up unexpectedly and in the most unreasonable places, and are, as likely as not, prepared for a banquet when you are not hungry and can't wait, and as cold and dark as a bushman's grave when you are and can.

Suddenly the driver said: "We're there now." He said this as if he had driven us to the scaffold to be hanged, and was fiercely glad that he'd got us there safely at last. We looked but saw nothing; then a light appeared ahead and seemed to come towards us; and presently we saw that it was a lantern held up by a man in a slouch hat, with a dark bushy beard, and a three-bushel bag around his shoulders. He held up his other hand, and said something to the driver in a tone that might have been used by the leader of a search party who had just found the body. The driver stopped and then went on slowly.

"What's up?" we asked. "What's the trouble?"

"Oh, it's all right," said the driver.

"The publican's wife is sick," somebody said, "and he wants us to come quietly."

The usual little slab and bark shanty was suggested in the gloom, with a big bark stable looming in the background. We climbed down like so many cripples. As soon as we began to feel our legs and be sure we had the right ones and the proper allowance of feet, we helped, as quietly as possible, to take the horses out and round to the stable.

"Is she very bad?" we asked the publican, showing as much concern as we could.

"Yes," he said, in a subdued voice of a rough man who had spent several anxious, sleepless nights by the sick bed of a dear one. "But, God willing, I think we'll pull her through."

Thus encouraged we said, sympathetically: "We're very sorry to trouble you, but I suppose we could manage to get a drink and a bit to eat?"

"Well," he said, "there's nothing to eat in the house, and I've only got rum and milk. You can have that if you like."

One of the pilgrims broke out here.

"Well of all the pubs," he began, "that I've ever—"

"Hush-sh-sh!" said the publican.

The pilgrim scowled and retired to the rear. You can't express your feelings freely when there's a woman dying close handy.

"Well, who says rum and milk?" asked the joker, in a low voice.

"Wait here," said the publican, and disappeared into the little front passage.

Presently a light showed through a window, with a scratched and fly-bitten B and A on two panes, and a mutilated R on the third, which was broken. A door opened, and we sneaked into the bar. It was like having drinks after hours where the police are strict and independent.

When we came out the driver was scratching his head and looking at the harness on the verandah floor.

"You fellows 'll have ter put in the time for an hour or so. The horses is out back somewheres," and he indicated the interior of Australia with a side jerk of his head, "and the boy ain't back with 'em yet."

"But dash it all," said the Pilgrim, "me and my mate—"

"Hush!" said the publican.

"How long are the horses likely to be?" we asked the driver.

"Dunno," he grunted. "Might be three or four hours. It's all accordin'."

"Now, look here," said the Pilgrim, "me and my mate wanter catch the train."

"Hush-sh-sh!" from the publican in a fierce whisper.

"Well, boss," said the joker, "can you let us have beds, then? I don't want to freeze here all night, anyway."

"Yes," said the landlord, "I can do that, but some of you will have to sleep double and some of you'll have to take it out of the sofas, and one or two 'll have to make a shakedown on the floor. There's plenty of bags in the stable, and you've got rugs and coats with you. Fix it up amongst yourselves."

"But look here!" interrupted the Pilgrim, desperately, "we can't afford to wait! We're only 'battlers', me and my mate, pickin' up crumbs by the wayside. We've got to catch the—"

"Hush!" said the publican, savagely. "You fool, didn't I tell you my missus was bad? I won't have any noise."

"But look here," protested the Pilgrim, "we must catch the train at Dead Camel—"

"You'll catch my boot presently," said the publican, with a savage oath, "and go further than Dead Camel. I won't have my missus disturbed for you or any other man! Just you shut up or get out, and take your blooming mate with you."

We lost patience with the Pilgrim and sternly took him aside.

"Now, for God's sake, hold your jaw," we said. "Haven't you got any consideration at all? Can't you see the man's wife is ill—dying perhaps—and he nearly worried off his head?"

The Pilgrim and his mate were scraggy little bipeds of the city push variety, so they were suppressed.

"Well," yawned the joker, "I'm not going to roost on a stump all night. I'm going to turn in."

"It'll be eighteenpence each," hinted the landlord. "You can settle now if you like to save time."

We took the hint, and had another drink. I don't know how we "fixed it up amongst ourselves," but we got settled down somehow. There was a lot of mysterious whispering and scuffling round by the light of a couple of dirty greasy bits of candle. Fortunately we dared not speak loud enough to have a row, though most of us were by this time in the humour to pick a quarrel with a long-lost brother.

The Joker got the best bed, as good-humoured, good-natured chaps generally do, without seeming to try for it. The growler of the party got the floor and chaff bags, as selfish men mostly do—without seeming to try for it either. I took it out of one of the "sofas", or rather that sofa took it out of me. It was short and narrow and down by the head, with a leaning to one corner on the outside, and had more nails and bits of gin-case than original sofa in it.

I had been asleep for three seconds, it seemed, when somebody shook me by the shoulder and said:

"Take yer seats."

When I got out, the driver was on the box, and the others were getting rum and milk inside themselves (and in bottles) before taking their seats.

It was colder and darker than before, and the South Pole seemed nearer, and pretty soon, but for the rum, we should have been in a worse fix than before.

There was a spell of grumbling. Presently someone said:

"I don't believe them horses was lost at all. I was round behind the stable before I went to bed, and seen horses there; and if they wasn't them same horses there, I'll eat 'em raw!"

"Would yer?" said the driver, in a disinterested tone.

"I would," said the passenger. Then, with a sudden ferocity, "and you too!"

The driver said nothing. It was an abstract question which didn't interest him.

We saw that we were on delicate ground, and changed the subject for a while. Then someone else said:

"I wonder where his missus was? I didn't see any signs of her about, or any other woman about the place, and we was pretty well all over it."

"Must have kept her in the stable," suggested the Joker.

"No, she wasn't, for Scotty and that chap on the roof was there after bags."

"She might have been in the loft," reflected the Joker.

"There was no loft," put in a voice from the top of the coach.

"I say, Mister—Mister man," said the Joker suddenly to the driver, "Was his missus sick at all?"

"I dunno," replied the driver. "She might have been. He said so, anyway. I ain't got no call to call a man a liar."

"See here," said the cannibalistic individual to the driver, in the tone of a man who has made up his mind for a row, "has that shanty-keeper got a wife at all?"

"I believe he has."

"And is she living with him?"

"No, she ain't—if yer wanter know."

"Then where is she?"

"I dunno. How am I to know? She left him three or four years ago. She was in Sydney last time I heard of her. It ain't no affair of mine, anyways."

"And is there any woman about the place at all, driver?" inquired a professional wanderer reflectively.

"No—not that I knows on. There useter be a old black gin come pottering round sometimes, but I ain't seen her lately."

"And excuse me, driver, but is there anyone round there at all?" enquired the professional wanderer, with the air of a conscientious writer, collecting material for an Australian novel from life, with an eye to detail.

"Naw," said the driver—and recollecting that he was expected to be civil and obliging to his employers' patrons, he added in surly apology, "Only the boss and the stableman, that I knows of." Then repenting of the apology, he asserted his manhood again, and asked, in a tone calculated to risk a breach of the peace, "Any more questions, gentlemen—while the shop's open?"

There was a long pause.

"Driver," asked the Pilgrim appealingly, "was them horses lost at all?"

"I dunno," said the driver. "He said they was. He's got the looking after them. It was nothing to do with me."

"Twelve drinks at sixpence a drink"—said the Joker, as if calculating to himself—"that's six bob, and, say on an average, four shouts—that's one pound four. Twelve beds at eighteenpence a bed—that's eighteen shillings; and say ten bob in various drinks and the stuff we brought with us, that's two pound twelve. That publican didn't do so bad out of us in two hours."

We wondered how much the driver got out of it, but thought it best not to ask him.

We didn't say much for the rest of the journey. There was the usual man who thought as much and knew all about it from the first, but he wasn't appreciated. We suppressed him. One or two wanted to go back and "stoush" that landlord, and the driver stopped the coach cheerfully at their request; but they said they'd come across him again and allowed themselves to be persuaded out of it. It made us feel bad to think how we had allowed ourselves to be delayed, and robbed, and had sneaked round on tiptoe, and how we had sat on the inoffensive Pilgrim and his mate, and all on account of a sick wife who didn't exist.

The coach arrived at Dead Camel in an atmosphere of mutual suspicion and distrust, and we spread ourselves over the train and departed.

A Gentleman Sharper and Steelman Sharper

Steelman and Smith had been staying at the hotel for several days in the dress and character of bushies down for what they considered a spree. The gentleman sharper from the Other Side had been hanging round them for three days now. Steelman was the more sociable, and, to all appearances, the greener of the two bush mates; but seemed rather too much under the influence of Smith, who was reserved, suspicious, self-contained, or sulky. He almost scowled at Gentleman Sharper's "Good-morning!" and "Fine day!", replied in monosyllables and turned half away with an uneasy, sullen, resentful hump of his shoulder and shuffle of his feet.

Steelman took Smith for a stroll on the round, bald tussock hills surrounding the city, and rehearsed him for the last act until after sundown.

Gentleman Sharper was lounging, with a cigar, on the end of the balcony, where he had been contentedly contemplating the beautiful death of day. His calm, classic features began to whiten (and sharpen) in the frosty moonlight.

Steelman and Smith sat on deck-chairs behind a half-screen of ferns on the other end of the balcony, smoked their after-dinner smoke, and talked in subdued tones as befitted the time and the scene— great, softened, misty hills in a semicircle, and the water and harbour lights in moonlight.

The other boarders were loitering over dinner, in their rooms, or gone out; the three were alone on the balcony, which was a rear one.

Gentleman Sharper moved his position, carelessly, noiselessly, yet quickly, until he leaned on the rail close to the ferns and could overhear every word the bushies said. He had dropped his cigar overboard, and his scented handkerchief behind a fern-pot en route.

"But he looks all right, and acts all right, and talks all right—and shouts all right," protested Steelman. "He's not stumped, for I saw twenty or thirty sovereigns when he shouted; and he doesn't seem to care a damn whether we stand in with him or not."

"There you are! That's just where it is!" said Smith, with some logic, but in a tone a wife uses in argument (which tone, by the way, especially if backed by logic or common sense, makes a man wild sooner than anything else in this world of troubles).

Steelman jerked his chair half-round in disgust. "That's you!" he snorted, "always suspicious! Always suspicious of everybody and everything! If I found myself shot into a world where I couldn't trust anybody I'd shoot myself out of it. Life would be worse than not worth living. Smith, you'll never make money, except by hard graft—hard, bullocking, nigger-driving graft like we had on that damned railway section for the last six months, up to our knees in water all winter, and all for a paltry cheque of one-fifty—twenty of that gone already. How do you expect to make money in this country if you won't take anything for granted, except hard cash? I tell you, Smith, there's a thousand pounds lost for every one gained or saved by trusting too little. How did Vanderbilt and—"

Steelman elaborated to a climax, slipping a glance warily, once or twice, out of the tail of his eye through the ferns, low down.

"There never was a fortune made that wasn't made by chancing it."

He nudged Smith to come to the point. Presently Smith asked, sulkily:

"Well, what was he saying?"

"I thought I told you! He says he's behind the scenes in this gold boom, and, if he had a hundred pounds ready cash to-morrow, he'd make three of it before Saturday. He said he could put one-fifty to one-fifty."

"And isn't he worth three hundred?"

"Didn't I tell you," demanded Steelman, with an impatient ring, and speaking rapidly, "that he lost his mail in the wreck of the 'Tasman'? You know she went down the day before yesterday, and the divers haven't got at the mails yet."

"Yes.... But why doesn't he wire to Sydney for some stuff?"

"I'm—! Well, I suppose I'll have to have patience with a born natural. Look here, Smith, the fact of the matter is that he's a sort of black-sheep—sent out on the remittance system, if the truth is known, and with letters of introduction to some big-bugs out here—that explains how he gets to know these wire-pullers behind the boom. His people have probably got the quarterly allowance business fixed hard and tight with a bank or a lawyer in Sydney; and there'll have to be enquiries about the lost 'draft' (as he calls a cheque) and a letter or maybe a cable home to England; and it might take weeks."

"Yes," said Smith, hesitatingly. "That all sounds right enough. But"—with an inspiration—"why don't he go to one of these big-bug boomsters he knows—that he got letters of introduction to—and get him to fix him up?"

"Oh, Lord!" exclaimed Steelman, hopelessly. "Listen to him! Can't you see that they're the last men he wants to let into his game? Why, he wants to use THEM! They're the mugs as far as he is concerned!"

"Oh—I see!" said Smith, after hesitating, and rather slowly—as if he hadn't quite finished seeing yet.

Steelman glanced furtively at the fern-screen, and nudged Smith again.

"He said if he had three hundred, he'd double it by Saturday?"

"That's what he said," replied Steelman, seeming by his tone to be losing interest in the conversation.

"And... well, if he had a hundred he could double that, I suppose."

"Yes. What are you driving at now?"

"If he had twenty—"

"Oh, God! I'm sick of you, Smith. What the—!"

"Hold on. Let me finish. I was only going to say that I'm willing to put up a fiver, and you put up another fiver, and if he doubles that for us then we can talk about standing in with him with a hundred—provided he can show his hundred."

After some snarling Steelman said: "Well, I'll try him! Now are you satisfied?"...

"He's moved off now," he added in a whisper; "but stay here and talk a bit longer."

Passing through the hall they saw Gentleman Sharper standing carelessly by the door of the private bar. He jerked his head in the direction of drinks. Steelman accepted the invitation—Smith passed on. Steelman took the opportunity to whisper to the Sharper—"I've been talking that over with my mate, and—"

"Come for a stroll," suggested the professional.

"I don't mind," said Steelman.

"Have a cigar?" and they passed out.

When they returned Steelman went straight to the room he occupied with Smith.

"How much stuff have we got, Smith?"

"Nine pounds seventeen and threepence."

Steelman gave an exclamation of disapproval with that state of financial affairs. He thought a second. "I know the barman here, and I think he knows me. I'll chew his lug for a bob or may be a quid."

Twenty minutes later he went to Gentleman Sharper's room with ten pounds—in very dirty Bank of New Zealand notes—such as those with which bush contractors pay their men.

Two mornings later the sharper suggested a stroll. Steelman went with him, with a face carefully made up to hear the worst.

After walking a hundred yards in a silence which might have been ominous—and was certainly pregnant—the sharper said:

"Well... I tried the water."

"Yes!" said Steelman in a nervous tone. "And how did you find it?"

"Just as warm as I thought. Warm for a big splash."

"How? Did you lose the ten quid?"

"Lose it! What did you take me for? I put ten to your ten as I told you I would. I landed 50 Pounds—"

"Fifty pounds for twenty?"

"That's the tune of it—and not much of a tune, either. My God! If I'd only had that thousand of mine by me, or even half of it, I'd have made a pile!"

"Fifty pounds for twenty!" cried Steelman excitedly. "Why, that's grand! And to think we chaps have been grafting like niggers all our lives! By God, we'll stand in with you for all we've got!"

"There's my hand on it," as they reached the hotel.

"If you come to my room I'll give you the 25 Pounds now, if you like."

"Oh, that's all right," exclaimed Steelman impulsively; "you mustn't think I don't—"

"That's all right. Don't you say any more about it. You'd best have the stuff to-night to show your mate."

"Perhaps so; he's a suspicious fool, but I made a bargain with him about our last cheque. He can hang on to the stuff, and I can't. If I'd been on my own I'd have blued it a week ago. Tell you what I'll do—we'll call our share (Smith's and mine) twenty quid. You take the odd fiver for your trouble."

"That looks fair enough. We'll call it twenty guineas to you and your mate. We'll want him, you know."

In his own and Smith's room Steelman thoughtfully counted twenty-one sovereigns on the toilet-table cover, and left them there in a pile.

He stretched himself, scratched behind his ear, and blinked at the money abstractedly. Then he asked, as if the thought just occurred to him: "By the way, Smith, do you see those yellow boys?"

Smith saw. He had been sitting on the bed with a studiously vacant expression. It was Smith's policy not to seem, except by request, to take any interest in, or, in fact, to be aware of anything unusual that Steelman might be doing—from patching his pants to reading poetry.

"There's twenty-one sovereigns there!" remarked Steelman casually.

"Yes?"

"Ten of 'em's yours."

"Thank yer, Steely."

"And," added Steelman, solemnly and grimly, "if you get taken down for 'em, or lose 'em out of the top-hole in your pocket, or spend so much as a shilling in riotous living, I'll stoush you, Smith."

Smith didn't seem interested. They sat on the beds opposite each other for two or three minutes, in something of the atmosphere that pervades things when conversation has petered out and the dinner-bell is expected to ring. Smith screwed his face and squeezed a pimple on his throat; Steelman absently counted the flies on the wall. Presently Steelman, with a yawning sigh, lay back on the pillow with his hands clasped under his head.

"Better take a few quid, Smith, and get that suit you were looking at the other day. Get a couple of shirts and collars, and some socks; better get a hat while you're at it—yours is a disgrace to your benefactor. And, I say, go to a chemist and get some cough stuff for that churchyarder of yours—we've got no use for it just now, and it makes me sentimental. I'll give you a cough when you want one. Bring me a syphon of soda, some fruit, and a tract."

"A what?"

"A tract. Go on. Start your boots."

While Smith was gone, Steelman paced the room with a strange, worried, haunted expression. He divided the gold that was left—(Smith had taken four pounds)—and put ten sovereigns in a pile on the extreme corner of the table. Then he walked up and down, up and down the room, arms tightly folded, and forehead knitted painfully, pausing abruptly now and then by the table to stare at the gold, until he heard Smith's step. Then his face cleared; he sat down and counted flies.

Smith was undoing and inspecting the parcels, having placed the syphon and fruit on the table. Behind his back Steelman hurriedly opened a leather pocketbook and glanced at the portrait of a woman and child and at the date of a post-office order receipt.

"Smith," said Steelman, "we're two honest, ignorant, green coves; hard-working chaps from the bush."

"Yes."

"It doesn't matter whether we are or not—we are as far as the world is concerned. Now we've grafted like bullocks, in heat and wet, for six months, and made a hundred and fifty, and come down to have a bit of a holiday before going back to bullock for another six months or a year. Isn't that so, Smith?"

"Yes."

"You could take your oath on it?"

"Yes."

"Well, it doesn't matter if it is so or not—it IS so, so far as the world is concerned. Now we've paid our way straight. We've always been pretty straight anyway, even if we are a pair of vagabonds, and I don't half like this new business; but it had to be done. If I hadn't taken down that sharper you'd have lost confidence in me and wouldn't have been able to mask your feelings, and I'd have had to stoush you. We're two hard-working, innocent bushies, down for an innocent spree, and we run against a cold-blooded professional sharper, a paltry sneak and a coward, who's got neither the brains nor the pluck to work in the station of life he togs himself for. He tries to do us out of our hard-earned little hundred and fifty—no matter whether we had it or not—and I'm obliged to take him down. Serve him right for a crawler. You haven't the least idea what I'm driving at, Smith, and that's the best of it. I've driven a nail of my life home, and no pincers ever made will get it out."

"Why, Steely, what's the matter with you?"

Steelman rose, took up the pile of ten sovereigns, and placed it neatly on top of the rest.

"Put the stuff away, Smith."

After breakfast next morning, Gentleman Sharper hung round a bit, and then suggested a stroll. But Steelman thought the weather looked too bad, so they went on the balcony for a smoke. They talked of the weather, wrecks, and things, Steelman leaning with his elbows on the balcony rail, and Sharper sociably and confidently in the same position close beside him. But the professional was evidently growing uneasy in his mind; his side of the conversation grew awkward and disjointed, and he made the blunder of drifting into an embarrassing silence before coming to the point. He took one elbow from the rail, and said, with a bungling attempt at carelessness which was made more transparent by the awkward pause before it:

"Ah, well, I must see to my correspondence. By the way, when could you make it convenient to let me have that hundred? The shares are starting up the last rise now, and we've got no time to lose if we want to double it."

Steelman turned his face to him and winked once—a very hard, tight, cold wink—a wink in which there was no humour: such a wink as Steelman had once winked at a half-drunken bully who was going to have a lark with Smith.

The sharper was one of those men who pull themselves together in a bad cause, as they stagger from the blow. But he wanted to think this time.

Later on he approached Steelman quietly and proposed partnership. But Steelman gave him to understand (as between themselves) that he wasn't taking on any pupils just then.

An Incident at Stiffner's

They called him "Stiffner" because he used, long before, to get a living by poisoning wild dogs near the Queensland border. The name stuck to him closer than misfortune did, for when he rose to the proud and independent position of landlord and sole proprietor of an out-back pub he was Stiffner still, and his place was "Stiffner's"—widely known.

They do say that the name ceased not to be applicable—that it fitted even better than in the old dingo days, but—well, they do say so. All we can say is that when a shearer arrived with a cheque, and had a drink or two, he was almost invariably seized with a desire to camp on the premises for good, spend his cheque in the shortest possible time, and forcibly shout for everything within hail—including the Chinaman cook and Stiffner's disreputable old ram.

The shanty was of the usual kind, and the scenery is as easily disposed of. There was a great grey plain stretching away from the door in front, and a mulga scrub from the rear; and in that scrub, not fifty yards from the kitchen door, were half a dozen nameless graves.

Stiffner was always drunk, and Stiffner's wife—a hard-featured Amazon—was boss. The children were brought up in a detached cottage, under the care of a "governess".

Stiffner had a barmaid as a bait for chequemen. She came from Sydney, they said, and her name was Alice. She was tall, boyishly handsome, and characterless; her figure might be described as "fine" or "strapping", but her face was very cold—nearly colourless. She was one of those selfishly sensual women—thin lips, and hard, almost vacant grey eyes; no thought of anything but her own pleasures, none for the man's. Some shearers would roughly call her "a squatter's girl". But she "drew"; she was handsome where women are scarce—very handsome, thought a tall, melancholy-looking jackeroo, whose evil spirit had drawn him to Stiffner's and the last shilling out of his pocket.

Over the great grey plain, about a fortnight before, had come "Old Danny", a station hand, for his semi-annual spree, and one "Yankee Jack" and his mate, shearers with horses, travelling for grass; and, about a week later, the Sydney jackeroo. There was also a sprinkling of assorted swagmen, who came in through the scrub and went out across the plain, or came in over the plain and went away through the scrub, according to which way their noses led them for the time being.

There was also, for one day, a tall, freckled native (son of a neighbouring "cocky"), without a thought beyond the narrow horizon within which he lived. He had a very big opinion of himself in a very small mind. He swaggered into the breakfast-room and round the table to his place with an expression of ignorant contempt on his phiz, his snub nose in the air and his under lip out. But during the meal he condescended to ask the landlord if he'd noticed that there horse that chap was ridin' yesterday; and Stiffner having intimated that he had, the native entertained the company with his opinion of that horse, and of a certain "youngster" he was breaking in at home, and divers other horses, mostly his or his father's, and of a certain cattle slut, &c.... He spoke at the landlord, but to the company, most of the time. After breakfast he swaggered round some more, but condescended to "shove" his hand into his trousers, "pull" out a "bob" and "chuck" it into the (blanky) hat for a pool. Those words express the thing better than any others we can think of. Finally, he said he must be off; and, there being no opposition to his departure, he chucked his saddle on to his horse, chucked himself into the saddle, said "s'long," and slithered off. And no one missed him.

Danny had been there a fortnight, and consequently his personal appearance was not now worth describing—it was better left alone, for the honour of the bush. His hobby was that he was the "stranger's friend", as he put it. He'd welcome "the stranger" and chum with him, and shout for him to an unlimited extent, and sympathise with him, hear of jobs or a "show" for him, assure him twenty times a day that he was his friend, give him hints and advice more or less worthless, make him drunk if possible, and keep him so while the cheque lasted; in short, Danny would do almost anything for the stranger except lend him a shilling, or give him some rations to carry him on. He'd promise that many times a day, but he'd sooner spend five pounds on drink for a man than give him a farthing.

Danny's cheque was nearly gone, and it was time he was gone too; in fact, he had received, and was still receiving, various hints to that effect, some of them decidedly pointed, especially the more recent ones. But Danny was of late becoming foolishly obstinate in his sprees, and less disposed to "git" when a landlord had done with him. He saw the hints plainly enough, but had evidently made up his mind to be doggedly irresponsive. It is a mistake to think that drink always dulls a man's feelings. Some natures are all the more keenly sensitive when alcoholically poisoned.

Danny was always front man at the shanty while his cheque was fresh—at least, so he was given to understand, and so he apparently understood. He was then allowed to say and do what he liked almost, even to mauling the barmaid about. There was scarcely any limit to the free and easy manner in which you could treat her, so long as your money lasted. She wouldn't be offended; it wasn't business to be so—"didn't pay." But, as soon as your title to the cheque could be decently shelved, you had to treat her like a lady. Danny knew this—none better; but he had been treated with too much latitude, and rushed to his destruction.

It was Sunday afternoon, but that made no difference in things at the shanty. Dinner was just over. The men were in the mean little parlour off the bar, interested in a game of cards, and Alice sat in one corner sewing. Danny was "acting the goat" round the fireplace; as ill-luck would have it, his attention was drawn to a basket of clean linen which stood on the side table, and from it, with sundry winks and grimaces, he gingerly lifted a certain garment of ladies' underwear—to put the matter decently. He held it up between his forefingers and thumbs, and cracked a rough, foolish joke—no matter what it was. The laugh didn't last long. Alice sprang to her feet, flinging her work aside, and struck a stage attitude—her right arm thrown out and the forefinger pointing rigidly, and rather crookedly, towards the door.

"Leave the room!" she snapped at Danny. "Leave the room! How dare you talk like that before me-e-ee!"

Danny made a step and paused irresolutely. He was sober enough to feel the humiliation of his position, and having once been a man of spirit, and having still the remnants of manhood about him, he did feel it. He gave one pitiful, appealing look at her face, but saw no mercy there. She stamped her foot again, jabbed her forefinger at the door, and said, "Go-o-o!" in a tone that startled the majority of the company nearly as much as it did Danny. Then Yankee Jack threw down his cards, rose from the table, laid his strong, shapely right hand—not roughly—on Danny's ragged shoulder, and engineered the drunk gently through the door.

"You's better go out for a while, Danny," he said; "there wasn't much harm in what you said, but your cheque's gone, and that makes all the difference. It's time you went back to the station. You've got to be careful what you say now."

When Jack returned to the parlour the barmaid had a smile for him; but he didn't take it. He went and stood before the fire, with his foot resting on the fender and his elbow on the mantelshelf, and looked blackly at a print against the wall before his face.

"The old beast!" said Alice, referring to Danny. "He ought to be kicked off the place!"

"HE'S AS GOOD AS YOU!"

The voice was Jack's; he flung the stab over his shoulder, and with it a look that carried all the contempt he felt.

She gasped, looked blankly from face to face, and witheringly at the back of Jack's head; but that didn't change colour or curl the least trifle less closely.

"Did you hear that?" she cried, appealing to anyone. "You're a nice lot o' men, you are, to sit there and hear a woman insulted, and not one of you man enough to take her part—cowards!"

The Sydney jackeroo rose impulsively, but Jack glanced at him, and he sat down again. She covered her face with her hands and ran hysterically to her room.

That afternoon another bushman arrived with a cheque, and shouted five times running at a pound a shout, and at intervals during the rest of the day when they weren't fighting or gambling.

Alice had "got over her temper" seemingly, and was even kind to the humble and contrite Danny, who became painfully particular with his "Thanky, Alice"—and afterwards offensive with his unnecessarily frequent threats to smash the first man who insulted her.

But let us draw the curtain close before that Sunday afternoon at Stiffner's, and hold it tight. Behind it the great curse of the West is in evidence, the chief trouble of unionism—drink, in its most selfish, barren, and useless form.

All was quiet at Stiffner's. It was after midnight, and Stiffner lay dead-drunk on the broad of his back on the long moonlit verandah, with all his patrons asleep around him in various grotesque positions. Stiffner's ragged grey head was on a cushion, and a broad maudlin smile on his red, drink-sodden face, the lower half of which was bordered by a dirty grey beard, like that of a frilled lizard. The red handkerchief twisted round his neck had a ghastly effect in the bright moonlight, making him look as if his throat was cut. The smile was the one he went to sleep with when his wife slipped the cushion under his head and thoughtfully removed the loose change from about his person. Near him lay a heap that was Danny, and spread over the bare boards were the others, some with heads pillowed on their swags, and every man about as drunk as his neighbour. Yankee Jack lay across the door of the barmaid's bedroom, with one arm bent under his head, the other lying limp on the doorstep, his handsome face turned out to the bright moonlight. The "family" were sound asleep in the detached cottage, and Alice— the only capable person on the premises—was left to put out the lamps and "shut up" for the night. She extinguished the light in the bar, came out, locked the door, and picked her way among and over the drunkards to the end of the verandah. She clasped her hands behind her head, stretched herself, and yawned, and then stood for a few moments looking out into the night, which softened the ragged line of mulga to right and left, and veiled the awful horizon of that great plain with which the "traveller" commenced, or ended, the thirty-mile "dry stretch". Then she moved towards her own door; before it she halted and stood, with folded arms, looking down at the drunken Adonis at her feet.

She breathed a long breath with a sigh in it, went round to the back, and presently returned with a buggy-cushion, which she slipped under his head—her face close to his—very close. Then she moved his arms gently off the threshold, stepped across him into her room, and locked the door behind her.

There was an uneasy movement in the heap that stood, or lay, for Danny. It stretched out, turned over, struggled to its hands and knees, and became an object. Then it crawled to the wall, against which it slowly and painfully up-ended itself, and stood blinking round for the water-bag, which hung from the verandah rafters in a line with its shapeless red nose. It staggered forward, held on by the cords, felt round the edge of the bag for the tot, and drank about a quart of water. Then it staggered back against the wall, stood for a moment muttering and passing its hand aimlessly over its poor ruined head, and finally collapsed into a shapeless rum-smelling heap and slept once more.

The jackeroo at the end of the verandah had awakened from his drunken sleep, but had not moved. He lay huddled on his side, with his head on the swag; the whole length of the verandah was before him; his eyes were wide open, but his face was in the shade. Now he rose painfully and stood on the ground outside, with his hands in his pockets, and gazed out over the open for a while. He breathed a long breath, too—with a groan in it. Then he lifted his swag quietly from the end of the floor, shouldered it, took up his water-bag and billy, and sneaked over the road, away from the place, like a thief. He struck across the plain, and tramped on, hour after hour, mile after mile, till the bright moon went down with a bright star in attendance and the other bright stars waned, and he entered the timber and tramped through it to the "cleared road", which stretched far and wide for twenty miles before him, with ghostly little dust-clouds at short intervals ahead, where the frightened rabbits crossed it. And still he went doggedly on, with the ghastly daylight on him—like a swagman's ghost out late. And a mongrel followed faithfully all the time unnoticed, and wondering, perhaps, at his master.

"What was yer doin' to that girl yesterday?" asked Danny of Yankee Jack next evening, as they camped on the far side of the plain. "What was you chaps sayin' to Alice? I heerd her cryin' in her room last night."

But they reckoned that he had been too drunk to hear anything except an invitation to come and have another drink; and so it passed.

The Hero of Redclay

The "boss-over-the-board" was leaning with his back to the wall between two shoots, reading a reference handed to him by a green-hand applying for work as picker-up or woolroller—a shed rouseabout. It was terribly hot. I was slipping past to the rolling-tables, carrying three fleeces to save a journey; we were only supposed to carry two. The boss stopped me:

"You've got three fleeces there, young man?"

"Yes."

Notwithstanding the fact that I had just slipped a light ragged fleece into the belly-wool and "bits" basket, I felt deeply injured, and righteously and fiercely indignant at being pulled up. It was a fearfully hot day.

"If I catch you carrying three fleeces again," said the boss quietly, "I'll give you the sack."

"I'll take it now if you like," I said.

He nodded. "You can go on picking-up in this man's place," he said to the jackeroo, whose reference showed him to be a non-union man—a "free-labourer", as the pastoralists had it, or, in plain shed terms, "a blanky scab". He was now in the comfortable position of a non-unionist in a union shed who had jumped into a sacked man's place.

Somehow the lurid sympathy of the men irritated me worse than the boss-over-the-board had done. It must have been on account of the heat, as Mitchell says. I was sick of the shed and the life. It was within a couple of days of cut-out, so I told Mitchell—who was shearing—that I'd camp up the Billabong and wait for him; got my cheque, rolled up my swag, got three days' tucker from the cook, said so-long to him, and tramped while the men were in the shed.

I camped at the head of the Billabong where the track branched, one branch running to Bourke, up the river, and the other out towards the Paroo—and hell.

About ten o'clock the third morning Mitchell came along with his cheque and his swag, and a new sheep-pup, and his quiet grin; and I wasn't too pleased to see that he had a shearer called "the Lachlan" with him.

The Lachlan wasn't popular at the shed. He was a brooding, unsociable sort of man, and it didn't make any difference to the chaps whether he had a union ticket or not. It was pretty well known in the shed— there were three or four chaps from the district he was reared in—that he'd done five years hard for burglary. What surprised me was that Jack Mitchell seemed thick with him; often, when the Lachlan was sitting brooding and smoking by himself outside the hut after sunset, Mitchell would perch on his heels alongside him and yarn. But no one else took notice of anything Mitchell did out of the common.

"Better camp with us till the cool of the evening," said Mitchell to the Lachlan, as they slipped their swags. "Plenty time for you to start after sundown, if you're going to travel to-night."

So the Lachlan was going to travel all night and on a different track. I felt more comfortable, and put the billy on. I did not care so much what he'd been or had done, but I was green and soft yet, and his presence embarrassed me.

They talked shearing, sheds, tracks, and a little unionism—the Lachlan speaking in a quiet voice and with a lot of sound, common sense, it seemed to me. He was tall and gaunt, and might have been thirty, or even well on in the forties. His eyes were dark brown and deep set, and had something of the dead-earnest sad expression you saw in the eyes of union leaders and secretaries—the straight men of the strikes of '90 and '91. I fancied once or twice I saw in his eyes the sudden furtive look of the "bad egg" when a mounted trooper is spotted near the shed; but perhaps this was prejudice. And with it all there was about the Lachlan something of the man who has lost all he had and the chances of all he was ever likely to have, and is past feeling, or caring, or flaring up—past getting mad about anything—something, all the same, that warned men not to make free with him.

He and Mitchell fished along the Billabong all the afternoon; I fished a little, and lay about the camp and read. I had an instinct that the Lachlan saw I didn't cotton on to his camping with us, though he wasn't the sort of man to show what he saw or felt. After tea, and a smoke at sunset, he shouldered his swag, nodded to me as if I was an accidental but respectful stranger at a funeral that belonged to him, and took the outside track. Mitchell walked along the track with him for a mile or so, while I poked round and got some boughs down for a bed, and fed and studied the collie pup that Jack had bought from the shearers' cook.

I saw them stop and shake hands out on the dusty clearing, and they seemed to take a long time about it; then Mitchell started back, and the other began to dwindle down to a black peg and then to a dot on the sandy plain, that had just a hint of dusk and dreamy far-away gloaming on it between the change from glaring day to hard, bare, broad moonlight.

I thought Mitchell was sulky, or had got the blues, when he came back; he lay on his elbow smoking, with his face turned from the camp towards the plain. After a bit I got wild—if Mitchell was going to go on like that he might as well have taken his swag and gone with the Lachlan. I don't know exactly what was the matter with me that day, and at last I made up my mind to bring the thing to a head.

"You seem mighty thick with the Lachlan," I said.

"Well, what's the matter with that?" asked Mitchell. "It ain't the first felon I've been on speaking terms with. I borrowed half-a-caser off a murderer once, when I was in a hole and had no one else to go to; and the murderer hadn't served his time, neither. I've got nothing against the Lachlan, except that he's a white man and bears a faint family resemblance to a certain branch of my tribe."

I rolled out my swag on the boughs, got my pipe, tobacco, and matches handy in the crown of a spare hat, and lay down.

Mitchell got up, re-lit his pipe at the fire, and mooned round for a while, with his hands behind him, kicking sticks out of the road, looking out over the plain, down along the Billabong, and up through the mulga branches at the stars; then he comforted the pup a bit, shoved the fire together with his toe, stood the tea-billy on the coals, and came and squatted on the sand by my head.

"Joe! I'll tell you a yarn."

"All right; fire away! Has it got anything to do with the Lachlan?"

"No. It's got nothing to do with the Lachlan now; but it's about a chap he knew. Don't you ever breathe a word of this to the Lachlan or anyone, or he'll get on to me."

"All right. Go ahead."

"You know I've been a good many things in my time. I did a deal of house-painting at one time; I was a pretty smart brush hand, and made money at it. Well, I had a run of work at a place called Redclay, on the Lachlan side. You know the sort of town—two pubs, a general store, a post office, a blacksmith's shop, a police station, a branch bank, and a dozen private weatherboard boxes on piles, with galvanized-iron tops, besides the humpies. There was a paper there, too, called the 'Redclay Advertiser' (with which was incorporated the 'Geebung Chronicle'), and a Roman Catholic church, a Church of England, and a Wesleyan chapel. Now you see more of private life in the house-painting line than in any other—bar plumbing and gasfitting; but I'll tell you about my house-painting experiences some other time.

"There was a young chap named Jack Drew editing the 'Advertiser' then. He belonged to the district, but had been sent to Sydney to a grammar school when he was a boy. He was between twenty-five and thirty; had knocked round a good deal, and gone the pace in Sydney. He got on as a boy reporter on one of the big dailies; he had brains and could write rings round a good many, but he got in with a crowd that called themselves 'Bohemians', and the drink got a hold on him. The paper stuck to him as long as it could (for the sake of his brains), but they had to sack him at last.

"He went out back, as most of them do, to try and work out their salvation, and knocked round amongst the sheds. He 'picked up' in one shed where I was shearing, and we carried swags together for a couple of months. Then he went back to the Lachlan side, and prospected amongst the old fields round there with his elder brother Tom, who was all there was left of his family. Tom, by the way, broke his heart digging Jack out of a cave in a drive they were working, and died a few minutes after the rescue. [] But that's another yarn. Jack Drew had a bad spree after that; then he went to Sydney again, got on his old paper, went to the dogs, and a Parliamentary push that owned some city fly-blisters and country papers sent him up to edit the 'Advertiser' at two quid a week. He drank again, and no wonder—you don't know what it is to run a 'Geebung Advocate' or 'Mudgee Budgee Chronicle', and live there. He was about the same build as the Lachlan, but stouter, and had something the same kind of eyes; but he was ordinarily as careless and devil-may-care as the Lachlan is grumpy and quiet.

"There was a doctor there, called Dr. Lebinski. They said he was a Polish exile. He was fifty or sixty, a tall man, with the set of an old soldier when he stood straight; but he mostly walked with his hands behind him, studying the ground. Jack Drew caught that trick off him towards the end. They were chums in a gloomy way, and kept to themselves—they were the only two men with brains in that town. They drank and fought the drink together. The Doctor was too gloomy and impatient over little things to be popular. Jack Drew talked too straight in the paper, and in spite of his proprietors—about pub spieling and such things—and was too sarcastic in his progress committee, town council, and toady reception reports. The Doctor had a hawk's nose, pointed grizzled beard and moustache, and steely-grey eyes with a haunted look in them sometimes (especially when he glanced at you sideways), as if he loathed his fellow men, and couldn't always hide it; or as if you were the spirit of morphia or opium, or a dead girl he'd wronged in his youth—or whatever his devil was, beside drink. He was clever, and drink had brought him down to Redclay.

"The bank manager was a heavy snob named Browne. He complained of being a bit dull of hearing in one ear—after you'd yelled at him three or four times; sometimes I've thought he was as deaf as a book-keeper in both. He had a wife and youngsters, but they were away on a visit while I was working in Redclay. His niece—or, rather, his wife's niece—a girl named Ruth Wilson, did the housekeeping. She was an orphan, adopted by her aunt, and was general slavey and scape-goat to the family—especially to the brats, as is often the case. She was rather pretty, and lady-like, and kept to herself. The women and girls called her Miss Wilson, and didn't like her. Most of the single men—and some of the married ones, perhaps—were gone on her, but hadn't the brains or the pluck to bear up and try their luck. I was gone worse than any, I think, but had too much experience or common sense. She was very good to me—used to hand me out cups of tea and plates of sandwiches, or bread and butter, or cake, mornings and afternoons the whole time I was painting the bank. The Doctor had known her people and was very kind to her. She was about the only woman—for she was more woman than girl—that he'd brighten up and talk for. Neither he nor Jack Drew were particularly friendly with Browne or his push.

"The banker, the storekeeper, one of the publicans, the butcher (a popular man with his hands in his pockets, his hat on the back of his head, and nothing in it), the postmaster, and his toady, the lightning squirter, were the scrub-aristocracy. The rest were crawlers, mostly pub spielers and bush larrikins, and the women were hags and larrikinesses. The town lived on cheque-men from the surrounding bush. It was a nice little place, taking it all round.

"I remember a ball at the local town hall, where the scrub aristocrats took one end of the room to dance in and the ordinary scum the other. It was a saving in music. Some day an Australian writer will come along who'll remind the critics and readers of Dickens, Carlyle, and Thackeray mixed, and he'll do justice to these little customs of ours in the little settled-district towns of Democratic Australia. This sort of thing came to a head one New Year's Night at Redclay, when there was a 'public' ball and peace on earth and good will towards all men—mostly on account of a railway to Redclay being surveyed. We were all there. They'd got the Doc. out of his shell to act as M.C.

"One of the aristocrats was the daughter of the local storekeeper; she belonged to the lawn-tennis clique, and they WERE select. For some reason or other—because she looked upon Miss Wilson as a slavey, or on account of a fancied slight, or the heat working on ignorance, or on account of something that comes over girls and women that no son of sin can account for—this Miss Tea-'n'-sugar tossed her head and refused Miss Wilson's hand in the first set and so broke the ladies' chain and the dance. Then there was a to-do. The Doctor held up his hand to stop the music, and said, very quietly, that he must call upon Miss So-and-so to apologise to Miss Wilson—or resign the chair. After a lot of fuss the girl did apologise in a snappy way that was another insult. Jack Drew gave Miss Wilson his arm and marched her off without a word—I saw she was almost crying. Some one said, 'Oh, let's go on with the dance.' The Doctor flashed round on them, but they were too paltry for him, so he turned on his heel and went out without a word. But I was beneath them again in social standing, so there was nothing to prevent me from making a few well-chosen remarks on things in general—which I did; and broke up that ball, and broke some heads afterwards, and got myself a good deal of hatred and respect, and two sweethearts; and lost all the jobs I was likely to get, except at the bank, the Doctor's, and the Royal.

"One day it was raining—general rain for a week. Rain, rain, rain, over ridge and scrub and galvanised iron and into the dismal creeks. I'd done all my inside work, except a bit under the Doctor's verandah, where he'd been having some patching and altering done round the glass doors of his surgery, where he consulted his patients. I didn't want to lose time. It was a Monday and no day for the Royal, and there was no dust, so it was a good day for varnishing. I took a pot and brush and went along to give the Doctor's doors a coat of varnish. The Doctor and Drew were inside with a fire, drinking whisky and smoking, but I didn't know that when I started work. The rain roared on the iron roof like the sea. All of a sudden it held up for a minute, and I heard their voices. The doctor had been shouting on account of the rain, and forgot to lower his voice. 'Look here, Jack Drew,' he said, 'there are only two things for you to do if you have any regard for that girl; one is to stop this' (the liquor I suppose he meant) 'and pull yourself together; and I don't think you'll do that—I know men. The other is to throw up the 'Advertiser'—it's doing you no good—and clear out.' 'I won't do that,' says Drew. 'Then shoot yourself,' said the Doctor. '(There's another flask in the cupboard). You know what this hole is like.... She's a good true girl—a girl as God made her. I knew her father and mother, and I tell you, Jack, I'd sooner see her dead than....' The roof roared again. I felt a bit delicate about the business and didn't like to disturb them, so I knocked off for the day.

"About a week before that I was down in the bed of the Redclay Creek fishing for 'tailers'. I'd been getting on all right with the housemaid at the 'Royal'—she used to have plates of pudding and hot pie for me on the big gridiron arrangement over the kitchen range; and after the third tuck-out I thought it was good enough to do a bit of a bear-up in that direction. She mentioned one day, yarning, that she liked a stroll by the creek sometimes in the cool of the evening. I thought she'd be off that day, so I said I'd go for a fish after I'd knocked off. I thought I might get a bite. Anyway, I didn't catch Lizzie—tell you about that some other time.

"It was Sunday. I'd been fishing for Lizzie about an hour when I saw a skirt on the bank out of the tail of my eye—and thought I'd got a bite, sure. But I was had. It was Miss Wilson strolling along the bank in the sunset, all by her pretty self. She was a slight girl, not very tall, with reddish frizzled hair, grey eyes, and small, pretty features. She spoke as if she had more brains than the average, and had been better educated. Jack Drew was the only young man in Redclay she could talk to, or who could talk to a girl like her; and that was the whole trouble in a nutshell. The newspaper office was next to the bank, and I'd seen her hand cups of tea and cocoa over the fence to his office window more than once, and sometimes they yarned for a while.

"She said, 'Good morning, Mr. Mitchell.'

"I said, 'Good morning, Miss.'

"There's some girls I can't talk to like I'd talk to other girls. She asked me if I'd caught any fish, and I said, 'No, Miss.' She asked me if it wasn't me down there fishing with Mr. Drew the other evening, and I said, 'Yes—it was me.' Then presently she asked me straight if he was fishing down the creek that afternoon? I guessed they'd been down fishing for each other before. I said, 'No, I thought he was out of town.' I knew he was pretty bad at the Royal. I asked her if she'd like to have a try with my line, but she said No, thanks, she must be going; and she went off up the creek. I reckoned Jack Drew had got a bite and landed her. I felt a bit sorry for her, too.

"The next Saturday evening after the rainy Monday at the Doctor's, I went down to fish for tailers—and Lizzie. I went down under the banks to where there was a big she-oak stump half in the water, going quietly, with an idea of not frightening the fish. I was just unwinding the line from my rod, when I noticed the end of another rod sticking out from the other side of the stump; and while I watched it was dropped into the water. Then I heard a murmur, and craned my neck round the back of the stump to see who it was. I saw the back view of Jack Drew and Miss Wilson; he had his arm round her waist, and her head was on his shoulder. She said, 'I WILL trust you, Jack—I know you'll give up the drink for my sake. And I'll help you, and we'll be so happy!' or words in that direction. A thunderstorm was coming on. The sky had darkened up with a great blue-black storm-cloud rushing over, and they hadn't noticed it. I didn't mind, and the fish bit best in a storm. But just as she said 'happy' came a blinding flash and a crash that shook the ridges, and the first drops came peltering down. They jumped up and climbed the bank, while I perched on the she-oak roots over the water to be out of sight as they passed. Half way to the town I saw them standing in the shelter of an old stone chimney that stood alone. He had his overcoat round her and was sheltering her from the wind...."

"Smoke-oh, Joe. The tea's stewing."

Mitchell got up, stretched himself, and brought the billy and pint-pots to the head of my camp. The moon had grown misty. The plain horizon had closed in. A couple of boughs, hanging from the gnarled and blasted timber over the billabong, were the perfect shapes of two men hanging side by side. Mitchell scratched the back of his neck and looked down at the pup curled like a glob of mud on the sand in the moonlight, and an idea struck him. He got a big old felt hat he had, lifted his pup, nose to tail, fitted it in the hat, shook it down, holding the hat by the brim, and stood the hat near the head of his doss, out of the moonlight. "He might get moonstruck," said Mitchell, "and I don't want that pup to be a genius." The pup seemed perfectly satisfied with this new arrangement.

"Have a smoke," said Mitchell. "You see," he added, with a sly grin, "I've got to make up the yarn as I go along, and it's hard work. It seems to begin to remind me of yarns your grandmother or aunt tells of things that happened when she was a girl—but those yarns are true. You won't have to listen long now; I'm well on into the second volume.

"After the storm I hurried home to the tent—I was batching with a carpenter. I changed my clothes, made a fire in the fire-bucket with shavings and ends of soft wood, boiled the billy, and had a cup of coffee. It was Saturday night. My mate was at the Royal; it was cold and dismal in the tent, and there was nothing to read, so I reckoned I might as well go up to the Royal, too, and put in the time.

"I had to pass the Bank on the way. It was the usual weatherboard box with a galvanised iron top—four rooms and a passage, and a detached kitchen and wash-house at the back; the front room to the right (behind the office) was the family bedroom, and the one opposite it was the living room. The 'Advertiser' office was next door. Jack Drew camped in a skillion room behind his printing office, and had his meals at the Royal. I noticed the storm had taken a sheet of iron off the skillion, and supposed he'd sleep at the Royal that night. Next to the 'Advertiser' office was the police station (still called the Police Camp) and the Courthouse. Next was the Imperial Hotel, where the scrub aristocrats went. There was a vacant allotment on the other side of the Bank, and I took a short cut across this to the Royal.

"They'd forgotten to pull down the blind of the dining-room window, and I happened to glance through and saw she had Jack Drew in there and was giving him a cup of tea. He had a bad cold, I remember, and I suppose his health had got precious to her, poor girl. As I glanced she stepped to the window and pulled down the blind, which put me out of face a bit—though, of course, she hadn't seen me. I was rather surprised at her having Jack in there, till I heard that the banker, the postmaster, the constable, and some others were making a night of it at the Imperial, as they'd been doing pretty often lately—and went on doing till there was a blow-up about it, and the constable got transferred Out Back. I used to drink my share then. We smoked and played cards and yarned and filled 'em up again at the Royal till after one in the morning. Then I started home.

"I'd finished giving the Bank a couple of coats of stone-colour that week, and was cutting in in dark colour round the spouting, doors, and window-frames that Saturday. My head was pretty clear going home, and as I passed the place it struck me that I'd left out the only varnish brush I had. I'd been using it to give the sashes a coat of varnish colour, and remembered that I'd left it on one of the window-sills—the sill of her bedroom window, as it happened. I knew I'd sleep in next day, Sunday, and guessed it would be hot, and I didn't want the varnish tool to get spoiled; so I reckoned I'd slip in through the side gate, get it, and take it home to camp and put it in oil. The window sash was jammed, I remember, and I hadn't been able to get it up more than a couple of inches to paint the runs of the sash. The grass grew up close under the window, and I slipped in quietly. I noticed the sash was still up a couple of inches. Just as I grabbed the brush I heard low voices inside—Ruth Wilson's and Jack Drew's—in her room.

"The surprise sent about a pint of beer up into my throat in a lump. I tip-toed away out of there. Just as I got clear of the gate I saw the banker being helped home by a couple of cronies.

"I went home to the camp and turned in, but I couldn't sleep. I lay think—think—thinking, till I thought all the drink out of my head. I'd brought a bottle of ale home to last over Sunday, and I drank that. It only made matters worse. I didn't know how I felt—I—well, I felt as if I was as good a man as Jack Drew—I—you see I've—you might think it soft—but I loved that girl, not as I've been gone on other girls, but in the old-fashioned, soft, honest, hopeless, far-away sort of way; and now, to tell the straight truth, I thought I might have had her. You lose a thing through being too straight or sentimental, or not having enough cheek; and another man comes along with more brass in his blood and less sentimental rot and takes it up—and the world respects him; and you feel in your heart that you're a weaker man than he is. Why, part of the time I must have felt like a man does when a better man runs away with his wife. But I'd drunk a lot, and was upset and lonely-feeling that night.

"Oh, but Redclay had a tremendous sensation next day! Jack Drew, of all the men in the world, had been caught in the act of robbing the bank. According to Browne's account in court and in the newspapers, he returned home that night at about twelve o'clock (which I knew was a lie, for I saw him being helped home nearer two) and immediately retired to rest (on top of the quilt, boots and all, I suppose). Some time before daybreak he was roused by a fancied noise (I suppose it was his head swelling); he rose, turned up a night lamp (he hadn't lit it, I'll swear), and went through the dining-room passage and office to investigate (for whisky and water). He saw that the doors and windows were secure, returned to bed, and fell asleep again.

"There is something in a deaf person's being roused easily. I know the case of a deaf chap who'd start up at a step or movement in the house when no one else could hear or feel it; keen sense of vibration, I reckon. Well, just at daybreak (to shorten the yarn) the banker woke suddenly, he said, and heard a crack like a shot in the house. There was a loose flooring-board in the passage that went off like a pistol-shot sometimes when you trod on it; and I guess Jack Drew trod on it, sneaking out, and he weighed nearly twelve stone. If the truth were known, he probably heard Browne poking round, tried the window, found the sash jammed, and was slipping through the passage to the back door. Browne got his revolver, opened his door suddenly, and caught Drew standing between the girl's door (which was shut) and the office door, with his coat on his arm and his boots in his hands. Browne covered him with his revolver, swore he'd shoot if he moved, and yelled for help. Drew stood a moment like a man stunned; then he rushed Browne, and in the struggle the revolver went off, and Drew got hit in the arm. Two of the mounted troopers—who'd been up looking to the horses for an early start somewhere—rushed in then, and took Drew. He had nothing to say. What could he say? He couldn't say he was a blackguard who'd taken advantage of a poor unprotected girl because she loved him. They found the back door unlocked, by the way, which was put down to the burglar; of course Browne couldn't explain that he came home too muddled to lock doors after him.

"And the girl? She shrieked and fell when the row started, and they found her like a log on the floor of her room after it was over.

"They found in Jack's overcoat pocket a parcel containing a cold chisel, small screw-wrench, file, and one or two other things that he'd bought that evening to tinker up the old printing press. I knew that, because I'd lent him a hand a few nights before, and he told me he'd have to get the tools. They found some scratches round the key-hole and knob of the office door that I'd made myself, scraping old splashes of paint off the brass and hand-plate so as to make a clean finish. Oh, it taught me the value of circumstantial evidence! If I was judge I wouldn't give a man till the 'risin' av the coort' on it, any more than I would on the bare word of the noblest woman breathing.

"At the preliminary examination Jack Drew said he was guilty. But it seemed that, according to law, he couldn't be guilty until after he was committed. So he was committed for trial at the next Quarter Sessions. The excitement and gabble were worse than the Dean case, or Federation, and sickened me, for they were all on the wrong track. You lose a lot of life through being behind the scenes. But they cooled down presently to wait for the trial.

"They thought it best to take the girl away from the place where she'd got the shock; so the Doctor took her to his house, where he had an old housekeeper who was as deaf as a post—a first class recommendation for a housekeeper anywhere. He got a nurse from Sydney to attend on Ruth Wilson, and no one except he and the nurse were allowed to go near her. She lay like dead, they said, except when she had to be held down raving; brain fever, they said, brought on by the shock of the attempted burglary and pistol shot. Dr. Lebinski had another doctor up from Sydney at his own expense, but nothing could save her—and perhaps it was as well. She might have finished her life in a lunatic asylum. They were going to send her to Sydney, to a brain hospital; but she died a week before the Sessions. She was right-headed for an hour, they said, and asking all the time for Jack. The Doctor told her he was all right and was coming—and, waiting and listening for him, she died.

"The case was black enough against Drew now. I knew he wouldn't have the pluck to tell the truth now, even if he was that sort of a man. I didn't know what to do, so I spoke to the Doctor straight. I caught him coming out of the Royal, and walked along the road with him a bit. I suppose he thought I was going to show cause why his doors ought to have another coat of varnish.

"'Hallo, Mitchell!' he said, 'how's painting?'

"'Doctor!' I said, 'what am I going to do about this business?'

"'What business?'

"'Jack Drew's.'

"He looked at me sideways—the swift haunted look. Then he walked on without a word, for half a dozen yards, hands behind, and studying the dust. Then he asked, quite quietly:

"'Do you know the truth?'

"'Yes!'

"About a dozen yards this time; then he said:

"'I'll see him in the morning, and see you afterwards,' and he shook hands and went on home.

"Next day he came to me where I was doing a job on a step ladder. He leaned his elbow against the steps for a moment, and rubbed his hand over his forehead, as if it ached and he was tired.

"'I've seen him, Mitchell,' he said.

"'Yes.'

"'You were mates with him, once, Out Back?'

"'I was.'

"'You know Drew's hand-writing?'

"'I should think so.'

"He laid a leaf from a pocketbook on top of the steps. I read the message written in pencil:

"'To Jack Mitchell.—We were mates on the track. If you know anything of my affair, don't give it away.—J. D.'

"I tore the leaf and dropped the bits into the paint-pot.

"'That's all right, Doctor,' I said; 'but is there no way?'

"'None.'

"He turned away, wearily. He'd knocked about so much over the world that he was past bothering about explaining things or being surprised at anything. But he seemed to get a new idea about me; he came back to the steps again, and watched my brush for a while, as if he was thinking, in a broody sort of way, of throwing up his practice and going in for house-painting. Then he said, slowly and deliberately:

"'If she—the girl—had lived, we might have tried to fix it up quietly. That's what I was hoping for. I don't see how we can help him now, even if he'd let us. He would never have spoken, anyway. We must let it go on, and after the trial I'll go to Sydney and see what I can do at headquarters. It's too late now. You understand, Mitchell?'

"'Yes. I've thought it out.'

"Then he went away towards the Royal.

"And what could Jack Drew or we do? Study it out whatever way you like. There was only one possible chance to help him, and that was to go to the judge; and the judge that happened to be on that circuit was a man who—even if he did listen to the story and believe it—would have felt inclined to give Jack all the more for what he was charged with. Browne was out of the question. The day before the trial I went for a long walk in the bush, but couldn't hit on anything that the Doctor might have missed.

"I was in the court—I couldn't keep away. The Doctor was there too. There wasn't so much of a change in Jack as I expected, only he had the gaol white in his face already. He stood fingering the rail, as if it was the edge of a table on a platform and he was a tired and bored and sleepy chairman waiting to propose a vote of thanks."

The only well-known man in Australia who reminds me of Mitchell is Bland Holt, the comedian. Mitchell was about as good hearted as Bland Holt, too, under it all; but he was bigger and roughened by the bush. But he seemed to be taking a heavy part to-night, for, towards the end of his yarn, he got up and walked up and down the length of my bed, dropping the sentences as he turned towards me. He'd folded his arms high and tight, and his face in the moonlight was—well, it was very different from his careless tone of voice. He was like—like an actor acting tragedy and talking comedy. Mitchell went on, speaking quickly—his voice seeming to harden:

"The charge was read out—I forget how it went—it sounded like a long hymn being given out. Jack pleaded guilty. Then he straightened up for the first time and looked round the court, with a calm, disinterested look—as if we were all strangers and he was noting the size of the meeting. And—it's a funny world, ain't it?—everyone of us shifted or dropped his eyes, just as if we were the felons and Jack the judge. Everyone except the Doctor; he looked at Jack and Jack looked at him. Then the Doctor smiled—I can't describe it—and Drew smiled back. It struck me afterwards that I should have been in that smile. Then the Doctor did what looked like a strange thing—stood like a soldier with his hands to Attention. I'd noticed that, whenever he'd made up his mind to do a thing, he dropped his hands to his sides: it was a sign that he couldn't be moved. Now he slowly lifted his hand to his forehead, palm out, saluted the prisoner, turned on his heel, and marched from the court-room. 'He's boozin' again,' someone whispered. 'He's got a touch of 'em.' 'My oath, he's ratty!' said someone else. One of the traps said:

"'Arder in the car-rt!'

"The judge gave it to Drew red-hot on account of the burglary being the cause of the girl's death and the sorrow in a respectable family; then he gave him five years' hard.

"It gave me a lot of confidence in myself to see the law of the land barking up the wrong tree, while only I and the Doctor and the prisoner knew it. But I've found out since then that the law is often the only one that knows it's barking up the wrong tree."

Mitchell prepared to turn in.

"And what about Drew," I asked.

"Oh, he did his time, or most of it. The Doctor went to headquarters, but either a drunken doctor from a geebung town wasn't of much account, or they weren't taking any romance just then at headquarters. So the Doctor came back, drank heavily, and one frosty morning they found him on his back on the bank of the creek, with his face like note-paper where the blood hadn't dried on it, and an old pistol in his hand—that he'd used, they said, to shoot Cossacks from horseback when he was a young dude fighting in the bush in Poland."

Mitchell lay silent a good while; then he yawned.

"Ah, well! It's a lonely track the Lachlan's tramping to-night; but I s'pose he's got his ghosts with him."

I'd been puzzling for the last half-hour to think where I'd met or heard of Jack Drew; now it flashed on me that I'd been told that Jack Drew was the Lachlan's real name.

I lay awake thinking a long time, and wished Mitchell had kept his yarn for daytime. I felt—well, I felt as if the Lachlan's story should have been played in the biggest theatre in the world, by the greatest actors, with music for the intervals and situations—deep, strong music, such as thrills and lifts a man from his boot soles. And when I got to sleep I hadn't slept a moment, it seemed to me, when I started wide awake to see those infernal hanging boughs with a sort of nightmare idea that the Lachlan hadn't gone, or had come back, and he and Mitchell had hanged themselves sociably—Mitchell for sympathy and the sake of mateship.

But Mitchell was sleeping peacefully, in spite of a path of moonlight across his face—and so was the pup.

The Darling River

The Darling—which is either a muddy gutter or a second Mississippi—is about six times as long as the distance, in a straight line, from its head to its mouth. The state of the river is vaguely but generally understood to depend on some distant and foreign phenomena to which bushmen refer in an off-hand tone of voice as "the Queenslan' rains", which seem to be held responsible, in a general way, for most of the out-back trouble.

It takes less than a year to go up stream by boat to Walgett or Bourke in a dry season; but after the first three months the passengers generally go ashore and walk. They get sick of being stuck in the same sort of place, in the same old way; they grow weary of seeing the same old "whaler" drop his swag on the bank opposite whenever the boat ties up for wood; they get tired of lending him tobacco, and listening to his ideas, which are limited in number and narrow in conception.

It shortens the journey to get out and walk; but then you will have to wait so long for your luggage— unless you hump it with you.

We heard of a man who determined to stick to a Darling boat and travel the whole length of the river. He was a newspaper man. He started on his voyage of discovery one Easter in flood-time, and a month later the captain got bushed between the Darling and South Australian border. The waters went away before he could find the river again, and left his boat in a scrub. They had a cargo of rations, and the crew stuck to the craft while the tucker lasted; when it gave out they rolled up their swags and went to look for a station, but didn't find one. The captain would study his watch and the sun, rig up dials and make out courses, and follow them without success. They ran short of water, and didn't smell any for weeks; they suffered terrible privations, and lost three of their number, NOT including the newspaper liar. There are even dark hints considering the drawing of lots in connection with something too terrible to mention. They crossed a thirty-mile plain at last, and sighted a black gin. She led them to a boundary rider's hut, where they were taken in and provided with rations and rum.

Later on a syndicate was formed to explore the country and recover the boat; but they found her thirty miles from the river and about eighteen from the nearest waterhole deep enough to float her, so they left her there. She's there still, or else the man that told us about it is the greatest liar Out Back.

Imagine the hull of a North Shore ferry boat, blunted a little at the ends and cut off about a foot below the water-line, and parallel to it, then you will have something shaped somewhat like the hull of a Darling mud-rooter. But the river boat is much stronger. The boat we were on was built and repaired above deck after the different ideas of many bush carpenters, of whom the last seemed by his work to have regarded the original plan with a contempt only equalled by his disgust at the work of the last carpenter but one. The wheel was boxed in, mostly with round sapling-sticks fastened to the frame with bunches of nails and spikes of all shapes and sizes, most of them bent. The general result was decidedly picturesque in its irregularity, but dangerous to the mental welfare of any passenger who was foolish enough to try to comprehend the design; for it seemed as though every carpenter had taken the opportunity to work in a little abstract idea of his own.

The way they "dock" a Darling River boat is beautiful for its simplicity. They choose a place where there are two stout trees about the boat's length apart, and standing on a line parallel to the river. They fix pulley-blocks to the trees, lay sliding planks down into the water, fasten a rope to one end of the steamer, and take the other end through the block attached to the tree and thence back aboard a second steamer; then they carry a rope similarly from the other end through the block on the second tree, and aboard a third boat. At a given signal one boat leaves for Wentworth, and the other starts for the Queensland border. The consequence is that craft number one climbs the bank amid the cheers of the local loafers, who congregate and watch the proceedings with great interest and approval. The crew pitch tents, and set to work on the hull, which looks like a big, rough shallow box.

We once travelled on the Darling for a hundred miles or so on a boat called the 'Mud Turtle'—at least, that's what WE called her. She might reasonably have haunted the Mississippi fifty years ago. She didn't seem particular where she went, or whether she started again or stopped for good after getting stuck. Her machinery sounded like a chapter of accidents and was always out of order, but she got along all the same, provided the steersman kept her off the bank.

Her skipper was a young man, who looked more like a drover than a sailor, and the crew bore a greater resemblance to the unemployed than to any other body we know of, except that they looked a little more independent. They seemed clannish, too, with an unemployed or free-labour sort of isolation. We have an idea that they regarded our personal appearance with contempt.

Above Louth we picked up a "whaler", who came aboard for the sake of society and tobacco. Not that he hoped to shorten his journey; he had no destination. He told us many reckless and unprincipled lies, and gave us a few ornamental facts. One of them took our fancy, and impressed us—with its beautiful simplicity, I suppose. He said: "Some miles above where the Darlin' and the Warrygo runs inter each other, there's a billygong runnin' right across between the two rivers and makin' a sort of tryhangular hyland; 'n' I can tel'yer a funny thing about it." Here he paused to light his pipe. "Now," he continued, impressively, jerking the match overboard, "when the Darlin's up, and the Warrygo's LOW, the billygong runs from the Darlin' into the WARRYGO; AND, when the Warrygo's up 'n' the Darlin's down, the waters runs FROM the Warrygo 'n' inter the Darlin'."

What could be more simple?

The steamer was engaged to go up a billabong for a load of shearers from a shed which was cutting out; and first it was necessary to tie up in the river and discharge the greater portion of the cargo in order that the boat might safely negotiate the shallow waters. A local fisherman, who volunteered to act as pilot, was taken aboard, and after he was outside about a pint of whisky he seemed to have the greatest confidence in his ability to take us to hell, or anywhere else—at least, he said so. A man was sent ashore with blankets and tucker to mind the wool, and we crossed the river, butted into the anabranch, and started out back. Only the Lord and the pilot know how we got there. We travelled over the bush, through its branches sometimes, and sometimes through grass and mud, and every now and then we struck something that felt and sounded like a collision. The boat slid down one hill, and "fetched" a stump at the bottom with a force that made every mother's son bite his tongue or break a tooth.

The shearers came aboard next morning, with their swags and two cartloads of boiled mutton, bread, "brownie", and tea and sugar. They numbered about fifty, including the rouseabouts. This load of sin sank the steamer deeper into the mud; but the passengers crowded over to port, by request of the captain, and the crew poked the bank away with long poles. When we began to move the shearers gave a howl like the yell of a legion of lost souls escaping from down below. They gave three cheers for the rouseabouts' cook, who stayed behind; then they cursed the station with a mighty curse. They cleared a space on deck, had a jig, and afterwards a fight between the shearers' cook and his assistant. They gave a mighty bush whoop for the Darling when the boat swung into that grand old gutter, and in the evening they had a general all-round time. We got back, and the crew had to reload the wool without assistance, for it bore the accursed brand of a "freedom-of-contract" shed.

We slept, or tried to sleep, that night on the ridge of two wool bales laid with the narrow sides up, having first been obliged to get ashore and fight six rounds with a shearer for the privilege of roosting there. The live cinders from the firebox went up the chimney all night, and fell in showers on deck. Every now and again a spark would burn through the "Wagga rug" of a sleeping shearer, and he'd wake suddenly and get up and curse. It was no use shifting round, for the wind was all ways, and the boat steered north, south, east, and west to humour the river. Occasionally a low branch would root three or four passengers off their wool bales, and they'd get up and curse in chorus. The boat started two snags; and towards daylight struck a stump. The accent was on the stump. A wool bale went overboard, and took a swag and a dog with it; then the owner of the swag and dog and the crew of the boat had a swearing match between them. The swagman won.

About daylight we stretched our cramped limbs, extricated one leg from between the wool bales, and found that the steamer was just crayfishing away from a mud island, where she had tied up for more wool. Some of the chaps had been ashore and boiled four or five buckets of tea and coffee. Shortly after the boat had settled down to work again an incident came along. A rouseabout rose late, and, while the others were at breakfast, got an idea into his head that a good "sloosh" would freshen him up; so he mooched round until he found a big wooden bucket with a rope to it. He carried the bucket aft of the wheel. The boat was butting up stream for all she was worth, and the stream was running the other way, of course, and about a hundred times as fast as a train. The jackeroo gave the line a turn round his wrist; before anyone could see him in time to suppress him, he lifted the bucket, swung it to and fro, and dropped it cleverly into the water.

This delayed us for nearly an hour. A couple of men jumped into the row boat immediately and cast her adrift. They picked up the jackeroo about a mile down the river, clinging to a snag, and when we hauled him aboard he looked like something the cat had dragged in, only bigger. We revived him with rum and got him on his feet; and then, when the captain and crew had done cursing him, he rubbed his head, went forward, and had a look at the paddle; then he rubbed his head again, thought, and remarked to his mates:

"Wasn't it lucky I didn't dip that bucket FOR'ARD the wheel?"

This remark struck us forcibly. We agreed that it was lucky—for him; but the captain remarked that it was damned unlucky for the world, which, he explained, was over-populated with fools already.

Getting on towards afternoon we found a barge loaded with wool and tied up to a tree in the wilderness. There was no sign of a man to be seen, nor any sign, except the barge, that a human being had ever been there. The captain took the craft in tow, towed it about ten miles up the stream, and left it in a less likely place than where it was before.

Floating bottles began to be more frequent, and we knew by that same token that we were nearing "Here's Luck!"—Bourke, we mean. And this reminds us.

When the Brewarrina people observe a more than ordinary number of bottles floating down the river, they guess that Walgett is on the spree; when the Louth chaps see an unbroken procession of dead marines for three or four days they know that Bourke's drunk. The poor, God-abandoned "whaler" sits in his hungry camp at sunset and watches the empty symbols of Hope go by, and feels more God-forgotten than ever—and thirstier, if possible—and gets a great, wide, thirsty, quaking, empty longing to be up where those bottles come from. If the townspeople knew how much misery they caused by their thoughtlessness they would drown their dead marines, or bury them, but on no account allow them to go drifting down the river, and stirring up hells in the bosoms of less fortunate fellow-creatures.

There came a man from Adelaide to Bourke once, and he collected all the empty bottles in town, stacked them by the river, and waited for a boat. What he wanted them for the legend sayeth not, but the people reckoned he had a "private still", or something of that sort, somewhere down the river, and were satisfied. What he came from Adelaide for, or whether he really did come from there, we do not know. All the Darling bunyips are supposed to come from Adelaide. Anyway, the man collected all the empty bottles he could lay his hands on, and piled them on the bank, where they made a good show. He waited for a boat to take his cargo, and, while waiting, he got drunk. That excited no comment. He stayed drunk for three weeks, but the townspeople saw nothing unusual in that. In order to become an object of interest in their eyes, and in that line, he would have had to stay drunk for a year and fight three times a day—oftener, if possible—and lie in the road in the broiling heat between whiles, and be walked on by camels and Afghans and free-labourers, and be locked up every time he got sober enough to smash a policeman, and try to hang himself naked, and be finally squashed by a loaded wool team.

But while he drank the Darling rose, for reasons best known to itself, and floated those bottles off. They strung out and started for the Antarctic Ocean, with a big old wicker-worked demijohn in the lead.

For the first week the down-river men took no notice; but after the bottles had been drifting past with scarcely a break for a fortnight or so, they began to get interested. Several whalers watched the procession until they got the jimjams by force of imagination, and when their bodies began to float down with the bottles, the down-river people got anxious.

At last the Mayor of Wilcannia wired Bourke to know whether Dibbs or Parkes was dead, or democracy triumphant, or if not, wherefore the jubilation? Many telegrams of a like nature were received during that week, and the true explanation was sent in reply to each. But it wasn't believed, and to this day Bourke has the name of being the most drunken town on the river.

After dinner a humorous old hard case mysteriously took us aside and said he had a good yarn which we might be able to work up. We asked him how, but he winked a mighty cunning wink and said that he knew all about us. Then he asked us to listen. He said:

"There was an old feller down the Murrumbidgee named Kelly. He was a bit gone here. One day Kelly was out lookin' for some sheep, when he got lost. It was gettin' dark. Bymeby there came an old crow in a tree overhead.

"'Kel-ley, you're lo-o-st! Kel-ley, you're lo-o-st!' sez the crow.

"'I know I am,' sez Kelly.

"'Fol-ler me, fol-ler me,' sez the crow.

"'Right y'are,' sez Kelly, with a jerk of his arm. 'Go ahead.'

"So the crow went on, and Kelly follered, an' bymeby he found he was on the right track.

"Sometime after Kelly was washin' sheep (this was when we useter wash the sheep instead of the wool). Kelly was standin' on the platform with a crutch in his hand landin' the sheep, when there came a old crow in the tree overhead.

"'Kelly, I'm hun-gry! Kel-ley, I'm hun-ger-ry!' sez the crow.

"'Alright,' sez Kelly; 'be up at the hut about dinner time 'n' I'll sling you out something.'

"'Drown—a—sheep! Drown—a—sheep, Kel-ley,' sez the crow.

"'Blanked if I do,' sez Kelly. 'If I drown a sheep I'll have to pay for it, be-God!'

"'Then I won't find yer when yer lost agin,' sez the crow.

"'I'm damned if yer will,' says Kelly. 'I'll take blanky good care I won't get lost again, to be found by a gory ole crow.'"

There are a good many fishermen on the Darling. They camp along the banks in all sorts of tents, and move about in little box boats that will only float one man. The fisherman is never heavy. He is mostly a withered little old madman, with black claws, dirty rags (which he never changes), unkempt hair and beard, and a "ratty" expression. We cannot say that we ever saw him catch a fish, or even get a bite, and we certainly never saw him offer any for sale.

He gets a dozen or so lines out into the stream, with the shore end fastened to pegs or roots on the bank, and passed over sticks about four feet high, stuck in the mud; on the top of these sticks he hangs bullock bells, or substitutes—jam tins with stones fastened inside to bits of string. Then he sits down and waits. If the cod pulls the line the bell rings.

The fisherman is a great authority on the river and fish, but has usually forgotten everything else, including his name. He chops firewood for the boats sometimes, but it isn't his profession—he's a fisherman. He is only sane on points concerning the river, though he has all the fisherman's eccentricities. Of course he is a liar.

When he gets his camp fixed on one bank it strikes him he ought to be over on the other, or at a place up round the bend, so he shifts. Then he reckons he was a fool for not stopping where he was before. He never dies. He never gets older, or drier, or more withered looking, or dirtier, or loonier—because he can't. We cannot imagine him as ever having been a boy, or even a youth. We cannot even try to imagine him as a baby. He is an animated mummy, who used to fish on the Nile three thousand years ago, and catch nothing.

We forgot to mention that there are wonderfully few wrecks on the Darling. The river boats seldom go down—their hulls are not built that way—and if one did go down it wouldn't sink far. But, once down, a boat is scarcely ever raised again; because, you see, the mud silts up round it and over it, and glues it, as it were, to the bottom of the river. Then the forty-foot alligators—which come down with the "Queenslan' rains", we suppose—root in the mud and fill their bellies with sodden flour and drowned deck-hands.

They tried once to blow up a wreck with dynamite because it (the wreck) obstructed navigation; but they blew the bottom out of the river instead, and all the water went through. The Government have been boring for it ever since. I saw some of the bores myself—there is one at Coonamble.

There is a yarn along the Darling about a cute Yankee who was invited up to Bourke to report on a proposed scheme for locking the river. He arrived towards the end of a long and severe drought, and was met at the railway station by a deputation of representative bushmen, who invited him, in the first place, to accompany them to the principal pub—which he did. He had been observed to study the scenery a good deal while coming up in the train, but kept his conclusions to himself. On the way to the pub he had a look at the town, and it was noticed that he tilted his hat forward very often, and scratched the back of his head a good deal, and pondered a lot; but he refrained from expressing an opinion—even when invited to do so. He guessed that his opinions wouldn't do much good, anyway, and he calculated that they would keep till he got back "over our way"—by which it was reckoned he meant the States.

When they asked him what he'd have, he said to Watty the publican:

"Wal, I reckon you can build me your national drink. I guess I'll try it."

A long colonial was drawn for him, and he tried it. He seemed rather startled at first, then he looked curiously at the half-empty glass, set it down very softly on the bar, and leaned against the same and fell into a reverie; from which he roused himself after a while, with a sorrowful jerk of his head.

"Ah, well," he said. "Show me this river of yourn."

They led him to the Darling, and he had a look at it.

"Is this your river?" he asked.

"Yes," they replied, apprehensively.

He tilted his hat forward till the brim nearly touched his nose, scratched the back of his long neck, shut one eye, and looked at the river with the other. Then, after spitting half a pint of tobacco juice into the stream, he turned sadly on his heel and led the way back to the pub. He invited the boys to "pisen themselves"; after they were served he ordered out the longest tumbler on the premises, poured a drop into it from nearly every bottle on the shelf, added a lump of ice, and drank slowly and steadily.

Then he took pity on the impatient and anxious population, opened his mouth, and spake.

"Look here, fellows," he drawled, jerking his arm in the direction of the river, "I'll tell you what I'll dew. I'll bottle that damned river of yourn in twenty-four hours!"

Later on he mellowed a bit, under the influence of several drinks which were carefully and conscientiously "built" from plans and specifications supplied by himself, and then, among other things, he said:

"If that there river rises as high as you say it dew—and if this was the States—why, we'd have had the Great Eastern up here twenty years ago"—or words to that effect.

Then he added, reflectively:

"When I come over here I calculated that I was going to make things hum, but now I guess I'll have to change my prospectus. There's a lot of loose energy laying round over our way, but I guess that if I wanted to make things move in your country I'd have to bring over the entire American nation—also his wife and dawg. You've got the makings of a glorious nation over here, but you don't get up early enough!"

The only national work performed by the blacks is on the Darling. They threw a dam of rocks across the river—near Brewarrina, we think—to make a fish trap. It's there yet. But God only knows where they got the stones from, or how they carried them, for there isn't a pebble within forty miles.

A Case for the Oracle

The Oracle and I were camped together. The Oracle was a bricklayer by trade, and had two or three small contracts on hand. I was "doing a bit of house-painting". There were a plasterer, a carpenter, and a plumber—we were all T'othersiders, and old mates, and we worked things together. It was in Westralia—the Land of T'othersiders—and, therefore, we were not surprised when Mitchell turned up early one morning, with his swag and an atmosphere of salt water about him.

He'd had a rough trip, he said, and would take a spell that day and take the lay of the land and have something cooked for us by the time we came home; and go to graft himself next morning. And next morning he went to work, "labouring" for the Oracle.

The Oracle and his mates, being small contractors and not pressed for time, had dispensed with the services of a labourer, and had done their own mixing and hod-carrying in turns. They didn't want a labourer now, but the Oracle was a vague fatalist, and Mitchell a decided one. So it passed.

The Oracle had a "Case" right under his nose—in his own employ, in fact; but was not aware of the fact until Mitchell drew his attention to it. The Case went by the name of Alfred O'Briar—which hinted a mixed parentage. He was a small, nervous working-man, of no particular colour, and no decided character, apparently. If he had a soul above bricks, he never betrayed it. He was not popular on the jobs. There was something sly about Alf, they said.

The Oracle had taken him on in the first place as a day-labourer, but afterwards shared the pay with him as with Mitchell. O'Briar shouted—judiciously, but on every possible occasion—for the Oracle; and, as he was an indifferent workman, the boys said he only did this so that the Oracle might keep him on. If O'Briar took things easy and did no more than the rest of us, at least one of us would be sure to get it into his head that he was loafing on us; and if he grafted harder than we did, we'd be sure to feel indignant about that too, and reckon that it was done out of nastiness or crawlsomeness, and feel a contempt for him accordingly. We found out accidentally that O'Briar was an excellent mimic and a bit of a ventriloquist, but he never entertained us with his peculiar gifts; and we set that down to churlishness.

O'Briar kept his own counsel, and his history, if he had one; and hid his hopes, joys, and sorrows, if he had any, behind a vacant grin, as Mitchell hid his behind a quizzical one. He never resented alleged satire—perhaps he couldn't see it—and therefore he got the name of being a cur. As a rule, he was careful with his money, and was called mean—not, however, by the Oracle, whose philosophy was simple, and whose sympathy could not realise a limit; nor yet by Mitchell. Mitchell waited.

O'Briar occupied a small tent by himself, and lived privately of evenings. When we began to hear two men talking at night in his tent, we were rather surprised, and wondered in a vague kind of way how any of the chaps could take sufficient interest in Alf to go in and yarn with him. In the days when he was supposed to be sociable, we had voted him a bore; even the Oracle was moved to admit that he was "a bit slow".

But late one night we distinctly heard a woman's voice in O'Briar's tent. The Oracle suddenly became hard of hearing, and, though we heard the voice on several occasions, he remained exasperatingly deaf, yet aggressively unconscious of the fact. "I have got enough to do puzzling over me own whys and wherefores," he said. Mitchell began to take some interest in O'Briar, and treated him with greater respect. But our camp had the name of being the best-constructed, the cleanest, and the most respectable in the vicinity. The health officer and constable in charge had complimented us on the fact, and we were proud of it. And there were three young married couples in camp, also a Darby and Joan; therefore, when the voice of a woman began to be heard frequently and at disreputable hours of the night in O'Briar's tent, we got uneasy about it. And when the constable who was on night duty gave us a friendly hint, Mitchell and I agreed that something must be done.

"Av coorse, men will be men," said the constable, as he turned his horse's head, "but I thought I'd mention it. O'Briar is a dacent man, and he's one of yer mates. Av coorse. There's a bad lot in that camp in the scrub over yander, and—av coorse. Good-day to ye, byes."

Next night we heard the voice in O'Briar's tent again, and decided to speak to Alf in a friendly way about it in the morning. We listened outside in the dark, but could not distinguish the words, though I thought I recognised the voice.

"It's the hussy from the camp over there; she's got holt of that fool, and she'll clean him out before she's done," I said. "We're Alf's mates, any way it goes, and we ought to put a stop to it."

"What hussy?" asked Mitchell; "there's three or four there."

"The one with her hair all over her head," I answered.

"Where else should it be?" asked Mitchell. "But I'll just have a peep and see who it is. There's no harm in that."

He crept up to the tent and cautiously moved the flap. Alf's candle was alight; he lay on his back in his bunk with his arms under his head, calmly smoking. We withdrew.

"They must have heard us," said Mitchell; "and she's slipped out under the tent at the back, and through the fence into the scrub."

Mitchell's respect for Alf increased visibly.

But we began to hear ominous whispers from the young married couples, and next Saturday night, which was pay-night, we decided to see it through. We did not care to speak to Alf until we were sure. He stayed in camp, as he often did, on Saturday evening, while the others went up town. Mitchell and I returned earlier than usual, and leaned on the fence at the back of Alf's tent.

We were scarcely there when we were startled by a "rat-tat-tat" as of someone knocking at a door. Then an old woman's voice INSIDE the tent asked: "Who's there?"

"It's me," said Alf's voice from the front, "Mr. O'Briar from Perth."

"Mary, go and open the door!" said the old woman. (Mitchell nudged me to keep quiet.)

"Come in, Mr. O'Breer," said the old woman. "Come in. How do you do? When did you get back?"

"Only last night," said Alf.

"Look at that now! Bless us all! And how did you like the country at all?"

"I didn't care much for it," said Alf. We lost the thread of it until the old woman spoke again.

"Have you had your tea, Mr. O'Breer?"

"Yes, thank you, Mrs. O'Connor."

"Are you quite sure, man?"

"Quite sure, thank you, Mrs. O'Connor." (Mitchell trod on my foot.)

"Will you have a drop of whisky or a glass of beer, Mr. O'Breer?"

"I'll take a glass of beer, thank you, Mrs. O'Connor."

There seemed to be a long pause. Then the old woman said, "Ah, well, I must get my work done, and Mary will stop here and keep you company, Mr. O'Breer." The arrangement seemed satisfactory to all parties, for there was nothing more said for a while. (Mitchell nudged me again, with emphasis, and I kicked his shin.)

Presently Alf said: "Mary!" And a girl's voice said, "Yes, Alf."

"You remember the night I went away, Mary?"

"Yes, Alf, I do."

"I have travelled long ways since then, Mary; I worked hard and lived close. I didn't make my fortune, but I managed to rub a note or two together. It was a hard time and a lonesome time for me, Mary. The summer's awful over there, and livin's bad and dear. You couldn't have any idea of it, Mary."

"No, Alf."

"I didn't come back so well off as I expected."

"But that doesn't matter, Alf."

"I got heart-sick and tired of it, and couldn't stand it any longer, Mary."

"But that's all over now, Alf; you mustn't think of it."

"Your mother wrote to me."

"I know she did" —(very low and gently).

"And do you know what she put in it, Mary?"

"Yes, Alf."

"And did you ask her to put it in?"

"Don't ask me, Alf."

"And it's all true, Mary?"

There was no answer, but the silence seemed satisfactory.

"And be sure you have yourself down here on Sunday, Alf, me son." ("There's the old woman come back!" said Mitchell.)

"An' since the girl's willin' to have ye, and the ould woman's willin'—there's me hand on it, Alf, me boy. An' God bless ye both." ("The old man's come now," said Mitchell.)

"Come along," said Mitchell, leading the way to the front of the tent.

"But I wouldn't like to intrude on them. It's hardly right, Mitchell, is it?"

"That's all right," said Mitchell. He tapped the tent pole.

"Come in," said Alf. Alf was lying on his bunk as before, with his arms under his head. His face wore a cheerful, not to say happy, expression. There was no one else in the tent. I was never more surprised in my life.

"Have you got the paper, Alf?" said Mitchell.

"Yes. You'll find it there at the foot of the bunk. There it is. Won't you sit down, Mitchell?"

"Not to-night," said Mitchell. "We brought you a bottle of ale. We're just going to turn in."

And we said "good-night". "Well," I said to Mitchell when we got inside, "what do you think of it?"

"I don't think of it at all," said Mitchell. "Do you mean to say you can't see it now?"

"No, I'm dashed if I can," I said. "Some of us must be drunk, I think, or getting rats. It's not to be wondered at, and the sooner we get out of this country the better."

"Well, you must be a fool, Joe," said Mitchell. "Can't you see? ALF THINKS ALOUD."

"WHAT?"

"Talks to himself. He was thinking about going back to his sweetheart. Don't you know he's a bit of a ventriloquist?"

Mitchell lay awake a long time, in the position that Alf usually lay in, and thought. Perhaps he thought on the same lines as Alf did that night. But Mitchell did his thinking in silence.

We thought it best to tell the Oracle quietly. He was deeply interested, but not surprised. "I've heerd of such cases before," he said. But the Oracle was a gentleman. "There's things that a man wants to keep to himself that ain't his business," he said. And we understood this remark to be intended for our benefit, and to indicate a course of action upon which the Oracle had decided, with respect to this case, and which we, in his opinion, should do well to follow.

Alf got away a week or so later, and we all took a holiday and went down to Fremantle to see him off. Perhaps he wondered why Mitchell gripped his hand so hard and wished him luck so earnestly, and was surprised when he gave him three cheers.

"Ah, well!" remarked Mitchell, as we turned up the wharf.

"I've heerd of such cases before," said the Oracle, meditatively. "They ain't common, but I've hear'd of such cases before."

A Daughter of Maoriland

A sketch of poor-class Maoris.

The new native-school teacher, who was "green", "soft", and poetical, and had a literary ambition, called her "August", and fondly hoped to build a romance on her character. She was down in the school registers as Sarah Moses, Maori, 16 years and three months. She looked twenty; but this was nothing, insomuch as the mother of the youngest child in the school—a dear little half-caste lady of two or three summers—had not herself the vaguest idea of the child's age, nor anybody else's, nor of ages in the abstract. The church register was lost some six years before, when "Granny", who was a hundred, if a day, was supposed to be about twenty-five. The teacher had to guess the ages of all the new pupils.

August was apparently the oldest in the school—a big, ungainly, awkward girl, with a heavy negro type of Maori countenance, and about as much animation, mentally or physically, as a cow. She was given to brooding; in fact, she brooded all the time. She brooded all day over her school work, but did it fairly well. How the previous teachers had taught her all she knew was a mystery to the new one. There had been a tragedy in August's family when she was a child, and the affair seemed to have cast a gloom over the lives of the entire family, for the lowering brooding cloud was on all their faces. August would take to the bush when things went wrong at home, and climb a tree and brood till she was found and coaxed home. Things, according to pa gossip, had gone wrong with her from the date of the tragedy, when she, a bright little girl, was taken—a homeless orphan—to live with a sister, and, afterwards, with an aunt-by-marriage. They treated her, 'twas said, with a brutality which must have been greatly exaggerated by pa-gossip, seeing that unkindness of this description is, according to all the best authorities, altogether foreign to Maori nature.

Pa-gossip—which is less reliable than the ordinary washerwoman kind, because of a deeper and more vicious ignorance—had it that one time when August was punished by a teacher (or beaten by her sister or aunt-by-marriage) she "took to the bush" for three days, at the expiration of which time she was found on the ground in an exhausted condition. She was evidently a true Maori or savage, and this was one of the reasons why the teacher with the literary ambition took an interest in her. She had a print of a portrait of a man in soldier's uniform, taken from a copy of the 'Illustrated London News', pasted over the fireplace in the whare where she lived, and neatly bordered by vandyked strips of silvered tea-paper. She had pasted it in the place of honour, or as near as she could get to it. The place of honour was sacred to framed representations of the Nativity and Catholic subjects, half-modelled, half-pictured. The print was a portrait of the last Czar of Russia, of all the men in the world; and August was reported to have said that she loved that man. His father had been murdered, so had her mother. This was one of the reasons why the teacher with the literary ambition thought he could get a romance out of her.

After the first week she hung round the new schoolmistress, dog-like—with "dog-like affection", thought the teacher. She came down often during the holidays, and hung about the verandah and back door for an hour or so; then, by-and-bye, she'd be gone. Her brooding seemed less aggressive on such occasions. The teacher reckoned that she had something on her mind, and wanted to open her heart to "the wife", but was too ignorant or too shy, poor girl; and he reckoned, from his theory of Maori character, that it might take her weeks, or months, to come to the point. One day, after a great deal of encouragement, she explained that she felt "so awfully lonely, Mrs. Lorrens." All the other girls were away, and she wished it was school-time.

She was happy and cheerful again, in her brooding way, in the playground. There was something sadly ludicrous about her great, ungainly figure slopping round above the children at play. The schoolmistress took her into the parlour, gave her tea and cake, and was kind to her; and she took it all with broody cheerfulness.

One Sunday morning she came down to the cottage and sat on the edge of the verandah, looking as wretchedly miserable as a girl could. She was in rags—at least, she had a rag of a dress on—and was barefooted and bareheaded. She said that her aunt had turned her out, and she was going to walk down the coast to Whale Bay to her grandmother—a long day's ride. The teacher was troubled, because he was undecided what to do. He had to be careful to avoid any unpleasantness arising out of Maori cliquism. As the teacher he couldn't let her go in the state she was in; from the depths of his greenness he trusted her, from the depths of his softness he pitied her; his poetic nature was fiercely indignant on account of the poor girl's wrongs, and the wife spoke for her. Then he thought of his unwritten romance, and regarded August in the light of copy, and that settled it. While he talked the matter over with his wife, August "hid in the dark of her hair," awaiting her doom. The teacher put his hat on, walked up to the pa, and saw her aunt. She denied that she had turned August out, but the teacher believed the girl. He explained his position, in words simplified for Maori comprehension, and the aunt and relations said they understood, and that he was "perfectly right, Mr. Lorrens." They were very respectful. The teacher said that if August would not return home, he was willing to let her stay at the cottage until such time as her uncle, who was absent, returned, and he (the teacher) could talk the matter over with him. The relations thought that that was the very best thing that could be done, and thanked him. The aunt, two sisters, and as many of the others, including the children, as were within sight or hail at the time— most of them could not by any possible means have had the slightest connection with the business in hand—accompanied the teacher to the cottage. August took to the flax directly she caught sight of her relations, and was with difficulty induced to return. There was a lot of talk in Maori, during which the girl and her aunt shuffled and swung round at the back of each other, and each talked over her shoulder, and laughed foolishly and awkwardly once or twice; but in the end the girl was sullenly determined not to return home, so it was decided that she should stay. The schoolmistress made tea.

August brightened from the first day. She was a different girl altogether. "I never saw such a change in a girl," said the young schoolmistress, and one or two others. "I always thought she was a good girl if taken the right way; all she wanted was a change and kind treatment." But the stolid old Maori chairman of the school committee only shrugged his shoulders and said (when the schoolmistress, woman-like, pressed him for an opinion to agree with her own), "You can look at it two ways, Mrs. Lorrens." Which, by the way, was about the only expression of opinion that the teacher was ever able to get out of him on any subject.

August worked and behaved well. She was wonderfully quick in picking up English ways and housework. True, she was awkward and not over cleanly in some things, but her mistress had patience with her. Who wouldn't have? She "couldn't do enough" for her benefactress; she hung on her words and sat at her footstool of evenings in a way that gladdened the teacher's sentimental nature; she couldn't bear to see him help his wife with a hat-pin or button—August must do it. She insisted on doing her mistress' hair every night. In short, she tried in every way to show her gratitude. The teacher and his wife smiled brightly at each other behind her back, and thought how cheerful the house was since she came, and wondered what they'd do without her. It was a settled thing that they should take her back to the city with them, and have a faithful and grateful retainer all their lives and a sort of Aunt Chloe for their children, when they had any. The teacher got yards of copy out of her for his "Maori Sketches and Characters", worked joyously at his romance, and felt great already, and was happy. She had a bed made up temporarily (until the teacher could get a spring mattress for her from town) on the floor in the dining-room, and when she'd made her bed she'd squat on it in front of the fire and sing Maori songs in a soft voice. She'd sing the teacher and his wife, in the next room, to sleep. Then she'd get up and have a feed, but they never heard her.

Her manners at the table (for she was treated "like one of themselves" in the broadest sense of the term) were surprisingly good, considering that the adults of her people were decidedly cow-like in white society, and scoffed sea-eggs, shell-fish, and mutton-birds at home with a gallop which was not edifying. Her appetite, it was true, was painful at times to the poetic side of the teacher's nature; but he supposed that she'd been half-starved at home, poor girl, and would get over it. Anyway, the copy he'd get out of her would repay him for this and other expenses a hundredfold. Moreover, begging and borrowing had ceased with her advent, and the teacher set this down to her influence.

The first jar came when she was sent on horseback to the town for groceries, and didn't get back till late the next day. She explained that some of her relations got hold of her and made her stay, and wanted her to go into public-houses with them, but she wouldn't. She said that SHE wanted to come home. But why didn't she? The teacher let it pass, and hoped she'd gain strength of character by-and-bye. He had waited up late the night before with her supper on the hob; and he and his wife had been anxious for fear something had happened to the poor girl who was under their care. He had walked to the treacherous river-ford several times during the evening, and waited there for her. So perhaps he was tired, and that was why he didn't write next night.

The sugar-bag, the onion-basket, the potato-bag and the tea-chest began to "go down" alarmingly, and an occasional pound of candles, a pigeon, a mutton-bird (plucked and ready for Sunday's cooking), and other little trifles went, also. August couldn't understand it, and the teacher believed her, for falsehood and deceit are foreign to the simple natures of the modern Maoris. There were no cats; but no score of ordinary cats could have given colour to the cat theory, had it been raised in this case. The breath of August advertised onions more than once, but no human stomach could have accounted for the quantity. She surely could not have eaten the other things raw—and she had no opportunities for private cooking, as far as the teacher and his wife could see. The other Maoris were out of the question; they were all strictly honest.

Thefts and annoyances of the above description were credited to the "swaggies" who infested the roads, and had a very bad name down that way; so the teacher loaded his gun, and told August to rouse him at once, if she heard a sound in the night. She said she would; but a heavy-weight "swaggie" could have come in and sat on her and had a smoke without waking her.

She couldn't be trusted to go a message. She'd take from three to six hours, and come back with an excuse that sounded genuine from its very simplicity. Another sister of hers lay ill in an isolated hut, alone and uncared for, except by the teacher's wife, and occasionally by a poor pa outcast who had negro blood in her veins, and a love for a white loafer. God help her! All of which sounds strange, considering that Maoris are very kind to each other. The schoolmistress sent August one night to stay with the sick Maori woman and help her as she could, and gave her strict instructions to come to the cottage first thing in the morning, and tell her how the sick woman was. August turned up at lunch-time next day. The teacher gave her her first lecture, and said plainly that he wasn't to be taken for a fool; then he stepped aside to get cool, and, when he returned, the girl was sobbing as if her heart would break, and the wife comforting her. She had been up all night, poor girl, and was thoroughly worn out. Somehow the teacher didn't feel uncomfortable about it. He went down to the whare. August had not touched a dishcloth or broom. She had slept, as she always did, like a pig, all night, while her sister lay and tossed in agony; in the morning she ate everything there was to eat in the house (which, it seemed, was the Maori way of showing sympathy in sickness and trouble), after which she brooded by the fire till the children, running out of school, announced the teacher's lunch hour.

August braced up again for a little while. The master thought of the trouble they had with Ayacanora in "Westward Ho", and was comforted, and tackled his romance again. Then the schoolmistress fell sick and things went wrong. The groceries went down faster than ever, and the house got very dirty, and began to have a native smell about it. August grew fat, and lazy, and dirty, and less reliable on washing-days, or when there was anything special to do in the house. "The savage blood is strong," thought the teacher, "and she is beginning to long for her own people and free unconventional life." One morning—on a washing-day, too, as it happened—she called out, before the teacher and his wife were up, that the Maoris who supplied them with milk were away, and she had promised to go up and milk the cow and bring the milk down. The teacher gave her permission. One of the scholars usually brought the milk early. Lunch time came and no August, no milk—strangest of all, only half the school children. The teacher put on his hat, and went up to the pa once more. He found August squatted in the midst of a circle of relations. She was entertaining them with one of a series of idealistic sketches of the teacher's domestic life, in which she showed a very vivid imagination, and exhibited an unaccountable savage sort of pessimism. Her intervals of absence had been occupied in this way from the first. The astounding slanders she had circulated concerning the teacher's private life came back, bit by bit, to his ears for a year afterwards, and her character sketches of previous teachers, and her own relations—for she spared nobody—would have earned a white woman a long and well-merited term of imprisonment for criminal libel. She had cunningly, by straightforward and unscrupulous lying, prejudiced the principal mother and boss woman of the pa against the teacher and his wife; as a natural result of which the old lady, who, like the rest, was very ignorant and ungrateful, "turned nasty" and kept the children from school. The teacher lost his temper, so the children were rounded up and hurried down to school immediately; with them came August and her aunt, with alleged explanations and excuses, and a shell-fish. The aunt and sisters said they'd have nothing to do with August. They didn't want her and wouldn't have her. The teacher said that, under those circumstances, she'd better go and drown herself; so she went home with them.

The whole business had been a plot by her nearest relations. They got rid of the trouble and expense of keeping her, and the bother of borrowing in person, whenever in need of trifles in the grocery line. Borrowing recommenced with her dismissal; but the teacher put a full stop to it, as far as he was concerned. Then August, egged on by her aunt, sent a blackguardly letter to the teacher's wife; the sick sister, by the way, who had been nursed and supplied with food by her all along, was in it, and said she was glad August sent the letter, and it served the schoolmistress right. The teacher went up to the pa once more; an hour later, August in person, accompanied, as usual, by a relation or two, delivered at the cottage an abject apology in writing, the composition of which would have discouraged the most enthusiastic advocate of higher education for the lower classes.

Then various petty annoyances were tried. The teacher is firmly convinced that certain animal-like sounds round the house at night were due to August's trying to find out whether his wife was as likely to be haunted as the Maoris were. He didn't dream of such a thing at the time, for he did not believe that one of them had the pluck to venture out after dark. But savage superstition must give way to savage hate. The girl's last "try-on" was to come down to the school fence, and ostentatiously sharpen a table-knife on the wires, while she scowled murderously in the direction of the schoolmistress, who was hanging out her washing. August looked, in her dark, bushy, Maori hair, a thoroughly wild savage. Her father had murdered her mother under particularly brutal circumstances, and the daughter took after her father.

The teacher called her and said: "Now, look here, my lady, the best thing you can do is to drop that nonsense at once" (she had dropped the knife in the ferns behind her), "for we're the wrong sort of people to try it on with. Now you get out of this and tell your aunt—she's sneaking there in the flax—what I tell you, and that she'd better clear out of this quick, or I'll have a policeman out and take the whole gang into town in an hour. Now be off, and shut that gate behind you, carefully, and fasten it." She did, and went.

The worst of it was that the August romance copy was useless. Her lies were even less reliable and picturesque than the common Jones Alley hag lie. Then the teacher thought of the soft fool he'd been, and that made him wild. He looked like a fool, and was one to a great extent, but it wasn't good policy to take him for one.

Strange to say, he and others had reason to believe that August respected him, and liked him rather than otherwise; but she hated his wife, who had been kind to her, as only a savage can hate. The younger pupils told the teacher, cheerfully and confidently, that August said she'd cut Mrs. Lorrens' throat the first chance she got. Next week the aunt sent down to ask if the teacher could sell her a bar of soap, and sent the same old shilling; he was tired of seeing it stuck out in front of him, so he took it, put it in his pocket, and sent the soap. This must have discouraged them, for the borrowing industry petered out. He saw the aunt later on, and she told him, cheerfully, that August was going to live with a half-caste in a certain house in town.

Poor August! For she was only a tool after all. Her "romance" was briefly as follows:—She went, per off-hand Maori arrangement, as 'housekeeper' in the hut of a labourer at a neighbouring saw-mill. She stayed three months, for a wonder; at the expiration of which time she put on her hat and explained that she was tired of stopping there, and was going home. He said, 'All right, Sarah, wait a while and I'll take you home.' At the door of her aunt's house he said, 'Well, good-bye, Sarah,' and she said, in her brooding way, 'Good-bye, Jim.' And that was all.

As the last apparent result of August's mischief-making, her brother or someone one evening rode up to the cottage, drunk and inclined to bluster. He was accompanied by a friend, also drunk, who came to see the fun, and was ready to use his influence on the winning side. The teacher went inside, brought out his gun, and slipped two cartridges in. "I've had enough of this," he said. "Now then, be off, you insolent blackguards, or I'll shoot you like rabbits. Go!" and he snapped his jaw and the breech of his gun together. As they rode off, the old local hawk happened to soar close over a dead lamb in the fern at the corner of the garden, and the teacher, who had been "laying" for him a long time, let fly both barrels at him, without thinking. When he turned, there was only a cloud of dust down the track.

The teacher taught that school for three years thereafter, without a hitch. But he went no more on Universal Brotherhood lines. And, for years after he had gone, his name was spoken of with great respect by the Maoris.

New Year's Night

It was dark enough for anything in Dead Man's Gap—a round, warm, close darkness, in which retreating sounds seemed to be cut off suddenly at a distance of a hundred yards or so, instead of growing faint and fainter, and dying away, to strike the ear once or twice again—and after minutes, it might seem—with startling distinctness, before being finally lost in the distance, as it is on clear, frosty nights. So with the sounds of horses' hoofs, stumbling on the rough bridle-track through the "saddle", the clatter of hoof-clipped stones and scrape of gravel down the hidden "siding", and the low sound of men's voices, blurred and speaking in monosyllables and at intervals it seemed, and in hushed, awed tones, as though they carried a corpse. To practical eyes, grown used to such a darkness, and at the nearest point, the passing blurs would have suggested two riders on bush hacks leading a third with an empty saddle on its back—a lady's or "side-saddle", if one could have distinguished the horns. They may have struck a soft track or level, or rounded the buttress of the hill higher up, but before they had time to reach or round the foot of the spur, blurs, whispers, stumble and clatter of hoofs, jingle of bridle rings, and the occasional clank together of stirrup irons, seemed shut off as suddenly and completely as though a great sound-proof door had swung to behind them.

It was dark enough on the glaringest of days down in the lonely hollow or "pocket", between two spurs, at the head of a blind gully behind Mount Buckaroo, where there was a more or less dusty patch, barely defined even in broad daylight by a spidery dog-legged fence on three sides, and a thin "two-rail" (dignified with the adjective "split-rail"—though rails and posts were mostly of saplings split in halves) running along the frontage. In about the middle of it a little slab hut, overshadowed by a big stringy-bark shed, was pointed out as Johnny Mears's Farm.

"Black as—as charcoal," said Johnny Mears. He had never seen coal, and was a cautious man, whose ideas came slowly. He stooped, close by the fence, with his hands on his knees, to "sky" the loom of his big shed and so get his bearings. He had been to have a look at the penned calves, and see that all slip-rails were up and pegged, for the words of John Mears junior, especially when delivered rapidly and shrilly and in injured tones, were not to be relied upon in these matters.

"It's hot enough to melt the belly out of my fiddle," said Johnny Mears to his wife, who sat on a three-legged stool by the rough table in the little whitewashed "end-room", putting a patch of patches over the seat of a pair of moleskin knickerbockers. He lit his pipe, moved a stool to the side of the great empty fireplace, where it looked cooler—might have been cooler on account of a possible draught suggested by the presence of the chimney, and where, therefore, he felt a breath cooler. He took his fiddle from a convenient shelf, tuned it slowly and carefully, holding his pipe (in his mouth) well up and to one side, as if the fiddle were an inquisitive and restless baby. He played "Little Drops o' Brandy" three times, right through, without variations, blinking solemnly the while; then he put the violin carefully back in its box, and started to cut up another pipeful.

"You should have gone, Johnny," said the haggard little woman.

"Rackin' the horse out a night like this," retorted Johnny, "and startin' ploughin' to-morrow. It ain't worth while. Let them come for me if they want me. Dance on a night like this! Why! they'll dance in—"

"But you promised. It won't do you no good, Johnny."

"It won't do me no harm."

The little woman went on stitching.

"It's smotherin' hot," said Johnny, with an impatient oath. "I don't know whether I'll turn in, or turn out, under the shed to-night. It's too d—d hot to roost indoors."

She bent her head lower over the patch. One smoked and the other stitched in silence for twenty minutes or so, during which time Johnny might be supposed to have been deliberating listlessly as to whether he'd camp out on account of the heat, or turn in. But he broke the silence with a clout at a mosquito on the nape of his neck, and a bad word.

"I wish you wouldn't swear so much, Johnny," she said wearily—"at least not to-night."

He looked at her blankly.

"Why—why to-night? What's the matter with you to-night, Mary? What's to-night more than any other night to you? I see no harm—can't a man swear when a mosquito sticks him?"

"I—I was only thinking of the boys, Johnny."

"The boys! Why, they're both on the hay in the shed." He stared at her again, shifted uneasily, crossed the other leg tightly, frowned, blinked, and reached for the matches. "You look a bit off-colour, Mary. It's the heat that makes us all a bit ratty at times. Better put that by and have a swill o' oatmeal and water, and turn in."

"It's too hot to go to bed. I couldn't sleep. I'm all right. I'll—I'll just finish this. Just reach me a drink from the water-bag—the pannikin's on the hob there, by your boot."

He scratched his head helplessly, and reached for the drink. When he sat down again, he felt strangely restless. "Like a hen that didn't know where to lay," he put it. He couldn't settle down or keep still, and didn't seem to enjoy his pipe somehow. He rubbed his head again.

"There's a thunderstorm comin'," he said. "That's what it is; and the sooner it comes the better."

He went to the back door, and stared at the blackness to the east, and, sure enough, lightning was blinking there.

"It's coming, sure enough; just hang out and keep cool for another hour, and you'll feel the difference."

He sat down again on the three-legged stool, folded his arms, with his elbows on his knees, drew a long breath, and blinked at the clay floor for a while; then he twisted the stool round on one leg, until he faced the old-fashioned spired wooden clock (the brass disc of the pendulum moving ghost-like through a scarred and scratched marine scene—Margate in England—on the glass that covered the lower half) that stood alone on the slab shelf over the fireplace. The hands indicated half-past two, and Johnny, who had studied that clock and could "hit the time nigh enough by it," after knitting his brows and blinking at the dial for a full minute by its own hand, decided "that it must be getting on toward nine o'clock."

It must have been the heat. Johnny stood up, raking his hair, turned to the door and back again, and then, after an impatient gesture, took up his fiddle and raised it to his shoulder. Then the queer thing happened. He said afterwards, under conditions favourable to such sentimental confidence, that a cold hand seemed to take hold of the bow, through his, and—anyway, before he knew what he was about he had played the first bars of "When First I Met Sweet Peggy", a tune he had played often, twenty years before, in his courting days, and had never happened to play since. He sawed it right through (the cold hand left after the first bar or two) standing up; then still stood with fiddle and bow trembling in his hands, with the queer feeling still on him, and a rush of old thoughts going through his head, all of which he set down afterwards to the effect of the heat. He put the fiddle away hastily, damning the bridge of it at the same time in loud but hurried tones, with the idea of covering any eccentricity which the wife might have noticed in his actions. "Must 'a' got a touch o' sun," he muttered to himself. He sat down, fumbled with knife, pipe, and tobacco, and presently stole a furtive glance over his shoulder at his wife.

The washed-out little woman was still sewing, but stitching blindly, for great tears were rolling down her worn cheeks.

Johnny, white-faced on account of the heat, stood close behind her, one hand on her shoulder and the other clenched on the table; but the clenched hand shook as badly as the loose one.

"Good God! What is the matter, Mary? You're sick!" (They had had little or no experience of illness.) "Tell me, Mary—come now! Has the boys been up to anything?"

"No, Johnny; it's not that."

"What is it then? You're taken sick! What have you been doing with yourself? It might be fever. Hold up a minute. You wait here quiet while I roost out the boys and send 'em for the doctor and someone—"

"No! no! I'm not sick, John. It's only a turn. I'll be all right in a minute."

He shifted his hand to her head, which she dropped suddenly, with a life-weary sigh, against his side.

"Now then!" cried Johnny, wildly, "don't you faint or go into disterricks, Mary! It'll upset the boys; think of the boys! It's only the heat—you're only takin' queer."

"It's not that; you ought to know me better than that. It was—I—Johnny, I was only thinking—we've been married twenty years to-night—an'—it's New Year's Night!"

"And I've never thought of it!" said Johnny (in the afterwards). "Shows what a God-forgotten selection will make of a man. She'd thought of it all the time, and was waiting for it to strike me. Why! I'd agreed to go and play at a darnce at Old Pipeclay School-house all night—that very night—and leave her at home because she hadn't asked to come; and it never struck me to ask her—at home by herself in that hole—for twenty-five bob. And I only stopped at home because I'd got the hump, and knew they'd want me bad at the school."

They sat close together on the long stool by the table, shy and awkward at first; and she clung to him at opening of thunder, and they started apart guiltily when the first great drops sounded like footsteps on the gravel outside, just as they'd done one night-time before—twenty years before.

If it was dark before, it was black now. The edge of the awful storm-cloud rushed up and under the original darkness like the best "drop" black-brushed over the cheap "lamp" variety, turning it grey by contrast. The deluge lasted only a quarter of an hour; but it cleared the night, and did its work. There was hail before it, too—big as emu eggs, the boys said—that lay feet deep in the old diggers' holes on Pipeclay for days afterwards—weeks some said.

The two sweethearts of twenty years ago and to-night watched the retreat of the storm, and, seeing Mount Buckaroo standing clear, they went to the back door, which opened opposite the end of the shed, and saw to the east a glorious arch of steel-blue, starry sky, with the distant peaks showing clear and blue away back under the far-away stars in the depth of it.

They lingered awhile—arms round each other's waists—before she called the boys, just as they had done this time of night twenty years ago, after the boys' grandmother had called her.

"Awlright, mother!" bawled back the boys, with unfilial independence of Australian youth. "We're awlright! We'll be in directly! Wasn't it a pelterer, mother?"

They went in and sat down again. The embarrassment began to wear off.

"We'll get out of this, Mary," said Johnny. "I'll take Mason's offer for the cattle and things, and take that job of Dawson's, boss or no boss"—(Johnny's bad luck was due to his inability in the past to "get on" with any boss for any reasonable length of time)—"I can get the boys on, too. They're doing no good here, and growing up. It ain't doing justice to them; and, what's more, this life is killin' you, Mary. That settles it! I was blind. Let the jumpt-up selection go! It's making a wall-eyed bullock of me, Mary—a dry-rotted rag of a wall-eyed bullock like Jimmy Nowlett's old Strawberry. And you'll live in town like a lady."

"Somebody coming!" yelled the boys.

There was a clatter of sliprails hurriedly thrown down, and clipped by horses' hoofs.

"Insoide there! Is that you, Johnny?"

"Yes!" ("I knew they'd come for you," said Mrs. Mears to Johnny.)

"You'll have to come, Johnny. There's no get out of it. Here's Jim Mason with me, and we've got orders to stun you and pack you if you show fight. The blessed fiddler from Mudgee didn't turn up. Dave Regan burst his concertina, and they're in a fix."

"But I can't leave the missus."

"That's all right. We've got the school missus's mare and side-saddle. She says you ought to be jolly well ashamed of yourself, Johnny Mears, for not bringing your wife on New Year's Night. And so you ought!"

Johnny did not look shame-faced, for reasons unknown to them.

"The boys couldn't find the horses," put in Mrs. Mears. "Johnny was just going down the gully again."

He gave her a grateful look, and felt a strange, new thrill of admiration for his wife.

"And—there's a bottle of the best put by for you, Johnny," added Pat McDurmer, mistaking Johnny's silence; "and we'll call it thirty bob!" (Johnny's ideas were coming slowly again, after the recent rush.) "Or—two quid!—there you are!"

"I don't want two quid, nor one either, for taking my wife to a dance on New Year's Night!" said Johnny Mears. "Run and put on your best bib and tucker, Mary."

And she hurried to dress as eager and excited, and smiling to herself as girlishly as she had done on such occasions on evenings before the bright New Year's Night twenty years ago.

Black Joe

They called him Black Joe, and me White Joe, by way of distinction and for the convenience of his boss (my uncle), and my aunt, and mother; so, when we heard the cry of "Bla-a-ack Joe!" (the adjective drawn out until it became a screech, after several repetitions, and the "Joe" short and sharp) coming across the flat in a woman's voice, Joe knew that the missus wanted him at the house, to get wood or water, or mind the baby, and he kept carefully out of sight; he went at once when uncle called. And when we heard the cry of "Wh-i-i-te Joe!" which we did with difficulty and after several tries—though Black Joe's ears were of the keenest—we knew that I was overdue at home, or absent without leave, and was probably in for a warming, as the old folk called it. On some occasions I postponed the warming as long as my stomach held out, which was a good while in five-corner, native-cherry, or yam season— but the warming was none the cooler for being postponed.

Sometimes Joe heard the wrong adjective, or led me to believe he did—and left me for a whole afternoon under the impression that the race of Ham was in demand at the homestead, when I myself was wanted there, and maternal wrath was increasing every moment of my absence.

But Joe knew that my conscience was not so elastic as his, and—well, you must expect little things like this in all friendships.

Black Joe was somewhere between nine and twelve when I first met him, on a visit to my uncle's station; I was somewhere in those years too. He was very black, the darker for being engaged in the interesting but uncertain occupation of "burning off" in his spare time—which wasn't particularly limited. He combined shepherding, 'possum and kangaroo hunting, crawfishing, sleeping, and various other occupations and engagements with that of burning off. I was very white, being a sickly town boy; but, as I took great interest in burning off, and was not particularly fond of cold water—it was in winter time— the difference in our complexions was not so marked at times.

Black Joe's father, old Black Jimmie, lived in a gunyah on the rise at the back of the sheepyards, and shepherded for my uncle. He was a gentle, good-humoured, easy-going old fellow with a pleasant smile; which description applies, I think, to most old blackfellows in civilisation. I was very partial to the old man, and chummy with him, and used to slip away from the homestead whenever I could, and squat by the campfire along with the other piccaninnies, and think, and yarn socially with Black Jimmie by the hour. I would give something to remember those conversations now. Sometimes somebody would be sent to bring me home, when it got too late, and Black Jimmie would say:

"Piccaninnie alonga possum rug," and there I'd be, sound asleep, with the other young Australians.

I liked Black Jimmie very much, and would willingly have adopted him as a father. I should have been quite content to spend my days in the scrub, enjoying life in dark and savage ways, and my nights "alonga possum rug"; but the family had other plans for my future.

It was a case of two blackfellows and one gin, when Black Jimmie went a-wooing—about twelve years before I made his acquaintance—and he fought for his bride in the black fashion. It was the last affair of that kind in the district. My uncle's brother professed to have been present at the fight, and gave me an alleged description of it. He said that they drew lots, and Black Jimmie put his hands on his knees and bent his head, and the other blackfellow hit him a whack on the skull with a nulla nulla. Then they had a nip of rum all round—Black Jimmie must have wanted it, for the nulla nulla was knotted, and heavy, and made in the most approved fashion. Then the other blackfellow bent his head, and Jimmie took the club and returned the whack with interest. Then the other fellow hit Jimmie a lick, and took a clout in return. Then they had another drink, and continued thus until Jimmie's rival lost all heart and interest in the business. But you couldn't take everything my uncle's brother said for granted.

Black Mary was a queen by right, and had the reputation of being the cleanest gin in the district; she was a great favourite with the squatters' wives round there. Perhaps she hoped to reclaim Jimmie—he was royal, too, but held easy views with regard to religion and the conventionalities of civilisation. Mary insisted on being married properly by a clergyman, made the old man build a decent hut, had all her children christened, and kept him and them clean and tidy up to the time of her death.

Poor Queen Mary was ambitious. She started to educate her children, and when they got beyond her— that is when they had learnt their letters—she was grateful for any assistance from the good-natured bush men and women of her acquaintance. She had decided to get her eldest boy into the mounted police, and had plans for the rest, and she worked hard for them, too. Jimmie offered no opposition, and gave her no assistance beyond the rations and money he earned shepherding—which was as much as could be expected of him.

He did as many husbands do "for the sake of peace and quietness"—he drifted along in the wake of his wife, and took things as easily as her schemes of reformation and education would allow him to.

Queen Mary died before her time, respected by all who knew or had heard of her. The nearest squatter's wife sent a pair of sheets for a shroud, with instructions to lay Mary out, and arranged (by bush telegraph) to drive over next morning with her sister-in-law and two other white women in the vicinity, to see Mary decently buried.

But the remnant of Jimmie's tribe were there beforehand. They tore the sheets in strips and tied Mary up in a bundle, with her chin to her knees—preparing her for burial in their own fashion—and mourned all night in whitewash and ashes. At least, the gins did. The white women saw that it was hopeless to attempt to untie any of the innumerable knots and double knots, even if it had been possible to lay Mary out afterwards; so they had to let her be buried as she was, with black and white obsequies. And we've got no interest in believing that she did not "jump up white woman" long ago.

My uncle and his brother took the two eldest boys. Black Jimmie shifted away from the hut at once with the rest of his family—for the "devil-devil" sat down there—and Mary's name was strictly "tabooed" in accordance with aboriginal etiquette.

Jimmie drifted back towards the graves of his fathers in company with a decreasing flock of sheep day by day (for the house of my uncle had fallen on times of drought and depression, and foot-rot and wool rings, and over-drafts and bank owners), and a few strips of bark, a dying fire, a black pipe, some greasy 'possum rugs and blankets, a litter of kangaroo tails, etc., four neglected piccaninnies, half a score of mangy mongrels, and, haply, a "lilly drap o' rum", by night.

The four little Australians grew dirtier and more shy and savage, and ate underdone kangaroo and 'possum and native bear, with an occasional treat of oak grubs and goanna by preference—and died out, one by one, as blacks do when brought within the ever widening circle of civilisation. Jimmie moved promptly after each death, and left the evil one in possession, and built another mia-mia—each one being less pretentious than the last. Finally he was left, the last of his tribe, to mourn his lot in solitude.

But the devil-devil came and sat down by King Jimmie's side one night, so he, too, moved out across the Old Man border, and the mia-mia rotted into the ground and the grass grew there.

I admired Joe; I thought him wiser and cleverer than any white boy in the world. He could smell out 'possums unerringly, and I firmly believed he could see yards through the muddiest of dam water; for once, when I dropped my boat in, and was not sure of the spot, he fished it out first try. With cotton reels and bits of stick and bark he would make the model of a station homestead, slaughter-yards, sheep-yards, and all complete, working in ideas and improvements of his own which might have been put into practice with advantage. He was a most original and interesting liar upon all subjects upon which he was ignorant and which came up incidentally. He gave me a very interesting account of an interview between his father and Queen Victoria, and mentioned casually that his father had walked across the Thames without getting wet.

He also told me how he, Joe, had tied a mounted trooper to a verandah post and thrashed him with pine saplings until the timber gave out and he was tired. I questioned Jimmie, but the incidents seemed to have escaped the old king's memory.

Joe could build bigger woodheaps with less wood than any black or white tramp or loafer round there. He was a born architect. He took a world of pains with his wood-heaps—he built them hollow, in the shape of a break-wind, with the convex side towards the house for the benefit of his employers. Joe was easy-going; he had inherited a love of peace and quietness from his father. Uncle generally came home after dark, and Joe would have little fires lit at safe distances all round the house, in order to convey an impression that the burning off was proceeding satisfactorily.

When the warm weather came, Joe and I got into trouble with an old hag for bathing in a waterhole in the creek in front of her shanty, and she impounded portions of our wardrobe. We shouldn't have lost much if she had taken it all; but our sense of injury was deep, especially as she used very bad grammar towards us.

Joe addressed her from the safe side of the water. He said, "Look here! Old leather-face, sugar-eye, plar-bag marmy, I call it you."

"Plar-bag marmy" meant "Mother Flour-bag", and ration sugar was decidedly muddy in appearance.

She came round the waterhole with a clothes prop, and made good time, too; but we got across and away with our clothes.

That little incident might have changed the whole course of my existence. Plar-bag Marmy made a formal complaint to uncle, who happened to pass there on horseback about an hour later; and the same evening Joe's latest and most carefully planned wood heap collapsed while aunt was pulling a stick out of it in the dark, and it gave her a bad scare, the results of which might have been serious.

So uncle gave us a thrashing, without the slightest regard for racial distinctions, and sent us to bed without our suppers.

We sought Jimmie's camp, but Joe got neither sympathy nor damper from his father, and I was sent home with a fatherly lecture "for going alonga that fella," meaning Joe.

Joe and I discussed existence at a waterhole down the creek next afternoon, over a billy of crawfish which we had boiled and a piece of gritty damper, and decided to retire beyond the settled districts—some five hundred miles or so—to a place that Joe said he knew of, where there were lagoons and billabongs ten miles wide, alive with ducks and fish, and black cockatoos and kangaroos and wombats, that only waited to be knocked over with a stick.

I thought I might as well start and be a blackfellow at once, so we got a rusty pan without a handle, and cooked about a pint of fat yellow oak-grubs; and I was about to fall to when we were discovered, and the full weight of combined family influence was brought to bear on the situation. We had broken a new pair of shears digging out those grubs from under the bark of the she-oaks, and had each taken a blade as his own especial property, which we thought was the best thing to do under the circumstances. Uncle wanted those shears badly, so he received us with the buggy whip—and he didn't draw the colour line either. All that night and next day I wished he had. I was sent home, and Joe went droving with uncle soon after that, else I might have lived a life of freedom and content and died out peacefully with the last of my adopted tribe.

Joe died of consumption on the track. When he was dying uncle asked: "Is there anything you would like?"

And Joe said: "I'd like a lilly drap o' rum, boss."

Which were his last words, for he drank the rum and died peacefully.

I was the first to hear the news at home, and, being still a youngster, I ran to the house, crying "Oh, mother! aunt's Joe is dead!"

There were visitors at our place at the time, and, as the eldest child of the maternal aunt in question had also been christened Joe—after a grandfather of our tribe (my tribe, not Black Joe's)—the news caused a sudden and unpleasant sensation. But cross-examination explained the mistake, and I retired to the rear of the pig-sty, as was my custom when things went wrong, with another cause for grief.

They Wait on the Wharf in Black

"Seems to me that honest, hard-working men seem to accumulate   the heaviest swags of trouble in this world."—Steelman.

Told by Mitchell's Mate.

We were coming back from West Australia, steerage—Mitchell, the Oracle, and I. I had gone over saloon, with a few pounds in my pocket. Mitchell said this was a great mistake—I should have gone over steerage with nothing but the clothes I stood upright in, and come back saloon with a pile. He said it was a very common mistake that men made, but, as far as his experience went, there always seemed to be a deep-rooted popular prejudice in favour of going away from home with a few pounds in one's pocket and coming back stumped; at least amongst rovers and vagabonds like ourselves—it wasn't so generally popular or admired at home, or in the places we came back to, as it was in the places we went to. Anyway it went, there wasn't the slightest doubt that our nearest and dearest friends were, as a rule, in favour of our taking away as little as we could possibly manage with, and coming back with a pile, whether we came back saloon or not; and that ought to settle the matter as far as any chap that had the slightest consideration for his friends or family was concerned.

There was a good deal of misery, underneath, coming home in that steerage. One man had had his hand crushed and amputated out Coolgardie way, and the stump had mortified, and he was being sent to Melbourne by his mates. Some had lost their money, some a couple of years of their life, some their souls; but none seemed to have lost the heart to call up the quiet grin that southern rovers, vagabonds, travellers for "graft" or fortune, and professional wanderers wear in front of it all. Except one man—an elderly eastern digger—he had lost his wife in Sydney while he was away.

They sent him a wire to the Boulder Soak, or somewhere out back of White Feather, to say that his wife was seriously ill; but the wire went wrong, somehow, after the manner of telegrams not connected with mining, on the lines of "the Western". They sent him a wire to say that his wife was dead, and that reached him all right—only a week late.

I can imagine it. He got the message at dinner-time, or when they came back to the camp. His mate wanted him to sit in the shade, or lie in the tent, while he got the billy boiled. "You must brace up and pull yourself together, Tom, for the sake of the youngsters." And Tom for long intervals goes walking up and down, up and down, by the camp—under the brassy sky or the gloaming—under the brilliant star-clusters that hang over the desert plain, but never raising his eyes to them; kicking a tuft of grass or a hole in the sand now and then, and seeming to watch the progress of the track he is tramping out. The wife of twenty years was with him—though two thousand miles away—till that message came.

I can imagine Tome sitting with his mates round the billy, they talking in quiet, subdued tones about the track, the departure of coaches, trains and boats—arranging for Tom's journey East, and the working of the claim in his absence. Or Tom lying on his back in his bunk, with his hands under his head and his eyes fixed on the calico above—thinking, thinking, thinking. Thinking, with a touch of his boyhood's faith perhaps; or wondering what he had done in his long, hard-working married life, that God should do this thing to him now, of all times.

"You'd best take what money we have in the camp, Tom; you'll want it all ag'in' the time you get back from Sydney, and we can fix it up arterwards.... There's a couple o' clean shirts o' mine—you'd best take 'em—you'll want 'em on the voyage.... You might as well take them there new pants o' mine, they'll only dry-rot out here—and the coat, too, if you like—it's too small for me, anyway. You won't have any time in Perth, and you'll want some decent togs to land with in Sydney."

"I wouldn't 'a' cared so much if I'd 'a' seen the last of her," he said, in a quiet, patient voice, to us one night by the rail. "I would 'a' liked to have seen the last of her."

"Have you been long in the West?"

"Over two years. I made up to take a run across last Christmas, and have a look at 'em. But I couldn't very well get away when 'exemption-time' came. I didn't like to leave the claim."

"Do any good over there?"

"Well, things brightened up a bit the last month or two. I had a hard pull at first; landed without a penny, and had to send back every shilling I could rake up to get things straightened up a bit at home. Then the eldest boy fell ill, and then the baby. I'd reckoned on bringing 'em over to Perth or Coolgardie when the cool weather came, and having them somewheres near me, where I could go and have a look at 'em now and then, and look after them."

"Going back to the West again?"

"Oh, yes. I must go for the sake of the youngsters. But I don't seem to have much heart in it." He smoked awhile. "Over twenty years we struggled along together—the missus and me—and it seems hard that I couldn't see the last of her. It's rough on a man."

"The world is damned rough on a man sometimes," said Mitchell, "most especially when he least deserves it."

The digger crossed his arms on the rail like an old "cocky" at the fence in the cool of the evening, yarning with an old crony.

"Mor'n twenty years she stuck to me and struggled along by my side. She never give in. I'll swear she was on her feet till the last, with her sleeves tucked up—bustlin' round.... And just when things was brightening and I saw a chance of giving her a bit of a rest and comfort for the end of her life.... I thought of it all only t'other week when things was clearing up ahead; and the last 'order' I sent over I set to work and wrote her a long letter, putting all the good news and encouragement I could think of into it. I thought how that letter would brighten up things at home, and how she'd read it round. I thought of lots of things that a man never gets time to think of while his nose is kept to the grindstone. And she was dead and in her grave, and I never knowed it."

Mitchell dug his elbow into my ribs and made signs for the matches to light his pipe.

"An' yer never knowed," reflected the Oracle.

"But I always had an idea when there was trouble at home," the digger went on presently, in his quiet, patient tone. "I always knowed; I always had a kind of feeling that way—I felt it—no matter how far I was away. When the youngsters was sick I knowed it, and I expected the letter that come. About a fortnight ago I had a feeling that way when the wife was ill. The very stars out there on the desert by the Boulder Soak seemed to say: 'There's trouble at home. Go home. There's trouble at home.' But I never dreamed what that trouble was. One night I did make up my mind to start in the morning, but when the morning came I hadn't an excuse, and was ashamed to tell my mates the truth. They might have thought I was going ratty, like a good many go out there." Then he broke off with a sort of laugh, as if it just struck him that we might think he was a bit off his head, or that his talk was getting uncomfortable for us. "Curious, ain't it?" he said.

"Reminds me of a case I knowed,—" commenced the Oracle, after a pause.

I could have pitched him overboard; but that was a mistake. He and the old digger sat on the for'ard hatch half the night yarning, mostly about queer starts, and rum go's, and curious cases the Oracle had knowed, and I think the Oracle did him a lot of good somehow, for he seemed more cheerful in the morning.

We were overcrowded in the steerage, but Mitchell managed to give up his berth to the old digger without letting him know it. Most of the chaps seemed anxious to make a place at the first table and pass the first helpings of the dishes to the "old cove that had lost his missus."

They all seemed to forget him as we entered the Heads; they had their own troubles to attend to. They were in the shadow of the shame of coming back hard up, and the grins began to grow faint and sickly. But I didn't forget him. I wish sometimes that I didn't take so much notice of things.

There was no mistaking them—the little group that stood apart near the end of the wharf, dressed in cheap black. There was the eldest single sister—thin, pale, and haggard-looking—that had had all the hard worry in the family till her temper was spoilt, as you could see by the peevish, irritable lines in her face. She had to be the mother of them all now, and had never known, perhaps, what it was to be a girl or a sweetheart. She gave a hard, mechanical sort of smile when she saw her father, and then stood looking at the boat in a vacant, hopeless sort of way. There was the baby, that he saw now for the first time, crowing and jumping at the sight of the boat coming in; there was the eldest boy, looking awkward and out of place in his new slop-suit of black, shifting round uneasily, and looking anywhere but at his father. But the little girl was the worst, and a pretty little girl she was, too; she never took her streaming eyes off her father's face the whole time. You could see that her little heart was bursting, and with pity for him. They were too far apart to speak to each other as yet. The boat seemed a cruel long long time swinging alongside—I wished they'd hurry up. He'd brought his traps up early, and laid 'em on the deck under the rail; he stood very quiet with his hands behind him, looking at his children. He had a strong, square, workman's face, but I could see his chin and mouth quivering under the stubbly, iron-grey beard, and the lump working in his throat; and one strong hand gripped the other very tight behind, but his eyelids never quivered—only his eyes seemed to grow more and more sad and lonesome. These are the sort of long, cruel moments when a man sits or stands very tight and quiet and calm-looking, with his whole past life going whirling through his brain, year after year, and over and over again. Just as the digger seemed about to speak to them he met the brimming eyes of his little girl turned up to his face. He looked at her for a moment, and then turned suddenly and went below as if pretending to go down for his things. I noticed that Mitchell—who hadn't seemed to be noticing anything in particular—followed him down. When they came on deck again we were right alongside.

"'Ello, Nell!" said the digger to the eldest daughter.

"'Ello, father!" she said, with a sort of gasp, but trying to smile.

"'Ello, Jack, how are you getting on?"

"All right, father," said the boy, brightening up, and seeming greatly relieved.

He looked down at the little girl with a smile that I can't describe, but didn't speak to her. She still stood with quivering chin and mouth and great brimming eyes upturned, full of such pity as I never saw before in a child-face—pity for him.

"You can get ashore now," said Mitchell; "see, they've got the gangway out aft."

Presently I saw Mitchell with the portmanteau in his hand, and the baby on his arm, steering them away to a quiet corner of the shed at the top of the wharf. The digger had the little girl in his arms, and both hers were round his neck, and her face hidden on his shoulder.

When Mitchell came back, he leant on the rail for a while by my side, as if it was a boundary fence out back, and there was no hurry to break up camp and make a start.

"What did you follow him below that time for, Mitchell?" I asked presently, for want of something better to say.

Mitchell looked at me out of the corners of his eyes.

"I wanted to score a drink!" he said. "I thought he wanted one and wouldn't like to be a Jimmy Woodser."

Seeing the Last of You

"When you're going away by boat," said Mitchell, "you ought to say good-bye to the women at home, and to the chaps at the last pub. I hate waiting on the wharf or up on deck when the boat's behind time. There's no sense in it, and a lot of unnecessary misery. Your friends wait on the wharf and you are kept at the rail to the bitter end, just when they and you most want a spell. And why? Some of them hang out because they love you, and want to see the last of you; some because they don't like you to see them going away without seeing the last of you; and you hang out mostly because it would hurt 'em if you went below and didn't give them a chance of seeing the last of you all the time—and you curse the boat and wish to God it would start. And those who love you most—the women-folk of the family—and who are making all the fuss and breaking their hearts about having to see the last of you, and least want to do it—they hang out the longest, and are the most determined to see it. Where's the sense in it? What's the good of seeing the last of you? How do women manage to get consolation out of a thing like that?

"But women get consolation out of queer things sometimes," he added reflectively, "and so do men.

"I remember when I was knocking about the coasts, an old aunt of mine always persisted in coming down to see the last of me, and bringing the whole family too—no matter if I was only going away for a month. I was her favourite. I always turned up again in a few months; but if I'd come back every next boat it wouldn't have made the slightest difference to her. She'd say that I mightn't come back some day, and then she'd never forgive herself nor the family for not seeing me off. I suppose she'll see the end of me yet if she lives long enough—and she's a wiry old lady of the old school. She was old-fashioned and dressed like a fright, they said at home. They hated being seen in public with her; to tell the truth, I felt a bit ashamed, too, at times. I wouldn't be, now. When I'd get her off on to the wharf I'd be overcome with my feelings, and have to retire to the privacy of the bar to hide my emotions till the boat was going. And she'd stand on the end of the pier and wave her handkerchief and mop her old eyes with it until she was removed by force.

"God bless her old heart! There wasn't so much affection wasted on me at home that I felt crowded by hers; and I never lost anything by her seeing the last of me.

"I do wish the Oracle would stop that confounded fiddle of his—it makes you think over damned old things."

Two Boys at Grinder Brothers'

Five or six half-grown larrikins sat on the cemented sill of the big window of Grinder Bros.' Railway Coach Factory waiting for the work bell, and one of the number was Bill Anderson—known as "Carstor Hoil"—a young terror of fourteen or fifteen.

"Here comes Balmy Arvie," exclaimed Bill as a pale, timid-looking little fellow rounded the corner and stood against the wall by the door. "How's your parents, Balmy?"

The boy made no answer; he shrank closer to the entrance. The first bell went.

"What yer got for dinner, Balmy? Bread 'n' treacle?" asked the young ruffian; then for the edification of his chums he snatched the boy's dinner bag and emptied its contents on the pavement.

The door opened. Arvie gathered up his lunch, took his time-ticket, and hurried in.

"Well, Balmy," said one of the smiths as he passed, "what do you think of the boat race?"

"I think," said the boy, goaded to reply, "that it would be better if young fellows of this country didn't think so much about racin' an' fightin'."

The questioner stared blankly for a moment, then laughed suddenly in the boy's face, and turned away. The rest grinned.

"Arvie's getting balmier than ever," guffawed young Bill.

"Here, Carstor Hoil," cried one of the smiths' strikers, "how much oil will you take for a chew of terbaccer?"

"Teaspoonful?"

"No, two."

"All right; let's see the chew, first."

"Oh, you'll get it. What yer frighten' of?... Come on, chaps, 'n' see Bill drink oil."

Bill measured out some machine oil and drank it. He got the tobacco, and the others got what they called "the fun of seein' Bill drink oil!"

The second bell rang, and Bill went up to the other end of the shop, where Arvie was already at work sweeping shavings from under a bench.

The young terror seated himself on the end of this bench, drummed his heels against the leg, and whistled. He was in no hurry, for his foreman had not yet arrived. He amused himself by lazily tossing chips at Arvie, who made no protest for a while. "It would be—better—for this country," said the young terror, reflectively and abstractedly, cocking his eye at the whitewashed roof beams and feeling behind him on the bench for a heavier chip—"it would be better—for this country—if young fellers didn't think so much about—about—racin'—AND fightin'."

"You let me alone," said Arvie.

"Why, what'll you do?" exclaimed Bill, bringing his eye down with feigned surprise. Then, in an indignant tone, "I don't mind takin' a fall out of yer, now, if yer like."

Arvie went on with his work. Bill tossed all the chips within reach, and then sat carelessly watching some men at work, and whistling the "Dead March". Presently he asked:

"What's yer name, Balmy?"

No answer.

"Carn't yer answer a civil question? I'd soon knock the sulks out of yer if I was yer father."

"My name's Arvie; you know that."

"Arvie what?"

"Arvie Aspinall."

Bill cocked his eye at the roof and thought a while and whistled; then he said suddenly:

"Say, Balmy, where d'yer live?"

"Jones' Alley."

"What?"

"Jones' Alley."

A short, low whistle from Bill. "What house?"

"Number Eight."

"Garn! What yer giv'nus?"

"I'm telling the truth. What's there funny about it? What do I want to tell you a lie for?"

"Why, we lived there once, Balmy. Old folks livin'?"

"Mother is; father's dead."

Bill scratched the back of his head, protruded his under lip, and reflected.

"I say, Arvie, what did yer father die of?"

"Heart disease. He dropped down dead at his work."

Long, low, intense whistle from Bill. He wrinkled his forehead and stared up at the beams as if he expected to see something unusual there. After a while he said, very impressively: "So did mine."

The coincidence hadn't done striking him yet; he wrestled with it for nearly a minute longer. Then he said:

"I suppose yer mother goes out washin'?"

"Yes."

"'N' cleans offices?"

"Yes."

"So does mine. Any brothers 'n' sisters?"

"Two—one brother 'n' one sister."

Bill looked relieved—for some reason.

"I got nine," he said. "Yours younger'n you?"

"Yes."

"Lot of bother with the landlord?"

"Yes, a good lot."

"Had any bailiffs in yet?"

"Yes, two."

They compared notes a while longer, and tailed off into a silence which lasted three minutes and grew awkward towards the end.

Bill fidgeted about on the bench, reached round for a chip, but recollected himself. Then he cocked his eye at the roof once more and whistled, twirling a shaving round his fingers the while. At last he tore the shaving in two, jerked it impatiently from him, and said abruptly:

"Look here, Arvie! I'm sorry I knocked over yer barrer yesterday."

"Thank you."

This knocked Bill out the first round. He rubbed round uneasily on the bench, fidgeted with the vise, drummed his fingers, whistled, and finally thrust his hands in his pockets and dropped on his feet.

"Look here, Arvie!" he said in low, hurried tones. "Keep close to me goin' out to-night, 'n' if any of the other chaps touches yer or says anything to yer I'll hit 'em!"

Then he swung himself round the corner of a carriage "body" and was gone.

Arvie was late out of the shop that evening. His boss was a sub-contractor for the coach-painting, and always tried to find twenty minutes' work for his boys just about five or ten minutes before the bell rang. He employed boys because they were cheap and he had a lot of rough work, and they could get under floors and "bogies" with their pots and brushes, and do all the "priming" and paint the trucks. His name was Collins, and the boys were called "Collins' Babies". It was a joke in the shop that he had a "weaning" contract. The boys were all "over fourteen", of course, because of the Education Act. Some were nine or ten—wages from five shillings to ten shillings. It didn't matter to Grinder Brothers so long as the contracts were completed and the dividends paid. Collins preached in the park every Sunday. But this has nothing to do with the story.

When Arvie came out it was beginning to rain and the hands had all gone except Bill, who stood with his back to a verandah-post, spitting with very fair success at the ragged toe of one boot. He looked up, nodded carelessly at Arvie, and then made a dive for a passing lorry, on the end of which he disappeared round the next corner, unsuspected by the driver, who sat in front with his pipe in his mouth and a bag over his shoulders.

Arvie started home with his heart and mind pretty full, and a stronger, stranger aversion to ever going back to the shop again. This new, unexpected, and unsought-for friendship embarrassed the poor lonely child. It wasn't welcome.

But he never went back. He got wet going home, and that night he was a dying child. He had been ill all the time, and Collins was one "baby" short next day.

The Selector's Daughter

I

She rode slowly down the steep siding from the main road to a track in the bed of the Long Gully, the old grey horse picking his way zig-zag fashion. She was about seventeen, slight in figure, and had a pretty freckled face with a pathetically drooping mouth, and big sad brown eyes. She wore a faded print dress, with an old black riding skirt drawn over it, and her head was hidden in one of those ugly, old-fashioned white hoods, which, seen from the rear, always suggest an old woman. She carried several parcels of groceries strapped to the front of the dilapidated side-saddle.

The track skirted a chain of rocky waterholes at the foot of the gully, and the girl glanced nervously at these ghastly, evil-looking pools as she passed them by. The sun had set, as far as Long Gully was concerned. The old horse carefully followed a rough bridle track, which ran up the gully now on one side of the watercourse and now on the other; the gully grew deeper and darker, and its sullen, scrub-covered sides rose more steeply as he progressed.

The girl glanced round frequently, as though afraid of someone following her. Once she drew rein, and listened to some bush sound. "Kangaroos," she murmured; it was only kangaroos. She crossed a dimmed little clearing where a farm had been, and entered a thick scrub of box and stringy-bark saplings. Suddenly with a heavy thud, thud, an "old man" kangaroo leapt the path in front, startling the girl fearfully, and went up the siding towards the peak.

"Oh, my God!" she gasped, with her hand on her heart.

She was very nervous this evening; her heart was hurt now, and she held her hand close to it, while tears started from her eyes and glistened in the light of the moon, which was rising over the gap ahead.

"Oh, if I could only go away from the bush!" she moaned.

The old horse plodded on, and now and then shook his head—sadly, it seemed—as if he knew her troubles and was sorry.

She passed another clearing, and presently came to a small homestead in a stringy-bark hollow below a great gap in the ridges—"Deadman's Gap". The place was called "Deadman's Hollow", and looked like it. The "house"—a low, two-roomed affair, with skillions—was built of half-round slabs and stringy-bark, and was nearly all roof; the bark, being darkened from recent rain, gave it a drearier appearance than usual.

A big, coarse-looking youth of about twenty was nailing a green kangaroo skin to the slabs; he was out of temper because he had bruised his thumb. The girl unstrapped the parcels and carried them in; as she passed her brother, she said:

"Take the saddle off for me, will you, Jack?"

"Oh, carnt yer take it off yerself?" he snarled; "carnt yer see I'm busy?"

She took off the saddle and bridle, and carried them into a shed, where she hung them on a beam. The patient old hack shook himself with an energy that seemed ill-advised, considering his age and condition, and went off towards the "dam".

An old woman sat in the main room beside a fireplace which took up almost the entire end of the house. A plank-table, supported on stakes driven into the ground, stood in the middle of the room, and two slab benches were fixtures on each side. The floor was clay. All was clean and poverty-stricken; all that could be whitewashed was white, and everything that could be washed was scrubbed. The slab shelves were covered with clean newspapers, on which bright tins, and pannikins, and fragments of crockery were set to the greatest advantage. The walls, however, were disfigured by Christmas supplements of illustrated journals.

The girl came in and sat down wearily on a stool opposite to the old woman.

"Are you any better, mother?" she asked.

"Very little, Mary, very little. Have you seen your father?"

"No."

"I wonder where he is?"

"You might wonder. What's the use of worrying about it, mother?"

"I suppose he's drinking again."

"Most likely. Worrying yourself to death won't help it!"

The old woman sat and moaned about her troubles, as old women do. She had plenty to moan about.

"I wonder where your brother Tom is? We haven't heard from him for a year now. He must be in trouble again; something tells me he must be in trouble again."

Mary swung her hood off into her lap.

"Why do you worry about it, mother? What's the use?"

"I only wish I knew. I only wish I knew!"

"What good would that do? You know Tom went droving with Fred Dunn, and Fred will look after him; and, besides, Tom's older now and got more sense."

"Oh, you don't care—you don't care! You don't feel it, but I'm his mother, and—"

"Oh, for God's sake, don't start that again, mother; it hurts me more than you think. I'm his sister; I've suffered enough, God knows! Don't make matters worse than they are!"

"Here comes father!" shouted one of the children outside, "'n' he's bringing home a steer."

The old woman sat still, and clasped her hands nervously. Mary tried to look cheerful, and moved the saucepan on the fire. A big, dark-bearded man, mounted on a small horse, was seen in the twilight driving a steer towards the cow-yard. A boy ran to let down the slip-rails.

Presently Mary and her mother heard the clatter of rails let down and put up again, and a minute later a heavy step like the tread of a horse was heard outside. The selector lumbered in, threw his hat in a corner, and sat down by the table. His wife rose and bustled round with simulated cheerfulness. Presently Mary hazarded—

"Where have you been, father?"

"Somewheers."

There was a wretched silence, lasting until the old woman took courage to say timidly:

"So you've brought a steer, Wylie?"

"Yes!" he snapped; the tone seemed defiant.

The old woman's hands trembled, so that she dropped a cup. Mary turned a shade paler.

"Here, git me some tea. Git me some TEA!" shouted Mr. Wylie. "I ain't agoin' to sit here all night!"

His wife made what haste her nervousness would allow, and they soon sat down to tea. Jack, the eldest son, was sulky, and his father muttered something about knocking the sulks out of him with an axe.

"What's annoyed you, Jack?" asked his mother, humbly.

He scowled and made no answer.

The younger children—three boys and a girl—began quarrelling as soon as they sat down. Wylie yelled at them now and then, and grumbled at the cooking, and at his wife for not being able to keep the children quiet. It was: "Marther! you didn't put no sugar in my tea." "Mother, Jimmy's got my place; make him move." "Mawther! do speak to this Fred." "Oh! father, this big brute of a Harry's kickin' me!" And so on.

II

When the miserable meal was over, Wylie got a rope and a butcher's knife, and went out to slaughter the steer; but first there was a row, because he thought—or pretended to think—that somebody had been using his knife. He lassoed the beast, drew it up to the rails, and slaughtered it.

Meanwhile, Jack and his next brother took an old gun, let the dogs loose, and went 'possum shooting.

Presently Wylie came in again, sat down by the fire, and smoked. The children quarrelled over a boy's book; Mrs. Wylie made weak attempts to keep the peace, but they took no notice of her. Suddenly her husband rose with an oath, seized the novel, and threw it behind the fire.

"Git to bed! git to bed!" he roared at the children; "git to bed, or I'll smash your brains with the axe!"

They got to bed. It was made of saplings and bark, covered with three bushel-bags full of straw and old pieces of blanket sewn together. The children quarrelled in bed till their father took off his belt and "went into" them, according to promise. There was a sudden hush, followed by a sound like a bird-clapper; then howls; then a peaceful calm fell upon that happy home.

Wylie went out again, and was absent an hour; on his return he sat by the fire and smoked sullenly. After a while he snatched the pipe from his mouth, and looked impatiently at the old woman.

"Oh! for God's sake, git to bed," he snapped, "and don't be asittin' there like a blarsted funeral! You're enough to give a man the dismals."

Mrs. Wylie gathered up her sewing and retired. Then he said to his daughter: "You come and hold the candle."

Mary put on her hood and followed her father to the yard. The carcase lay close to the rails, against which two sheets of bark had been raised as a break-wind. The beast had been partly skinned, and a portion of the hide, where a brand might have been, was carefully turned back. Mary noticed this at once. Her father went on with his work, and occasionally grumbled at her for not holding the candle right.

"Where did you buy the steer, father?" she asked.

"Ask no questions and hear no lies." Then he added, "Carn't you see it's a clear skin?"

She had a keen sense of humour, and the idea of a "'clear skin' steer" would have amused her at any other time. She didn't smile now.

He turned the carcase over; the loose hide fell back, and the light shone on a distinct brand. White as a sheet went Mary's face, and her hand trembled so that she nearly let the candle fall.

"What are you adoin' of now?" shouted her father. "Hold the candle, carn't you? You're worse than the old woman."

"Father! the beast is branded! See!— What does PB stand for?"

"Poor Beggar, like myself. Hold the candle, carn't you?—and hold your tongue."

Mary was startled again by hearing the tread of a horse, but it was only the old grey munching round. Her father finished skinning, and drew the carcase up to a make-shift "gallows". "Now you can go to bed," he said, in a gentler tone.

She went to her bedroom—a small, low, slab skillion, built on to the end of the house—and fell on her knees by the bunk.

"God help me! God help us all!" she cried.

She lay down, but could not sleep. She was nervously ill—nearly mad, because of the dark, disgraceful cloud of trouble which hung over her home. Always in trouble—always in trouble. It started long ago, when her favourite brother Tom ran away. She was little more than a child then, intensely sensitive; and when she sat in the old bark school she fancied that the other children were thinking or whispering to each other, "Her brother's in prison! Mary Wylie's brother's in prison! Tom Wylie's in gaol!" She was thinking of it still. They were ever with her, those horrible days and nights of the first shadow of shame. She had the same horror of evil, the same fearful dread of disgrace that her mother had. She had been ambitious; she had managed to read much, and had wild dreams of going to the city and rising above the common level, but that was all past now.

How could she rise when the cruel hand of disgrace was ever ready to drag her down at any moment. "Ah, God!" she moaned in her misery, "if we could only be born without kin—with no one to disgrace us but ourselves! It's cruel, God, it's cruel to suffer for the crimes of others!" She was getting selfish in her troubles—like her mother. "I want to go away from the bush and all I know.... O God, help me to go away from the bush!" Presently she fell asleep—if sleep it may be called—and dreamt of sailing away, sailing away far out on the sea beyond the horizon of her dread. Then came a horrible nightmare, in which she and all her family were arrested for a terrible crime. She woke in a fright, and saw a reddish glare on the window. Her father was poking round some logs where they had been "burning-off". A pungent odour came through a broken pane and turned her sick. He was burning the hide.

Wylie did not go to bed that night; he got his breakfast before daylight, and rode up through the frosty gap while the stars were still out, carrying a bag of beef in front of him on the grey horse. Mary said nothing about the previous night. Her mother wondered how much "father" had given for the steer, and supposed he had gone into town to sell the hide; the poor soul tried to believe that he had come by the steer honestly. Mary fried some meat, and tried to eat it for her mother's sake, but could manage only a few mouthfuls. Mrs. Wylie also seemed to have lost her appetite. Jack and his brother, who had been out all night, made a hearty breakfast. Then Jimmy started to peg out the 'possum skins, while Jack went to look for a missing pony. Mary was left to milk all the cows, and feed the calves and pigs.

Shortly after dinner one of the children ran to the door, and cried:

"Why, mother—here's three mounted troopers comin' up the gully!"

"Oh, my God!" cried the mother, sinking back in her chair and trembling like a leaf. The children ran and hid in the scrub. Mary stood up, terribly calm, and waited. The eldest trooper dismounted, came to the door, glanced suspiciously at the remains of the meal, and abruptly asked the dreaded question:

"Mrs. Wylie, where's your husband?"

She dropped the tea-cup, from which she had pretended to be drinking unconcernedly.

"What? Why, what do you want my husband for?" she asked in pitiful desperation. SHE looked like the guilty party.

"Oh, you know well enough," he sneered impatiently.

Mary rose and faced him. "How dare you talk to my mother like that?" she cried. "If my poor brother Tom was only here—you—you coward!"

The youngest trooper whispered something to his senior, and then, stung by a sharp retort, said:

"Well, you needn't be a pig."

His two companions passed through into the spare skillion, where they found some beef in a cask, and more already salted down under a bag on the end of a bench; then they went out at the back and had a look at the cow-yard. The younger trooper lingered behind.

"I'll try and get them up the gully on some excuse," he whispered to Mary. "You plant the hide before we come back."

"It's too late. Look there!" She pointed through the doorway.

The other two were at the logs where the fire had been; the burning hide had stuck to the logs in places like glue.

"Wylie's a fool," remarked the old trooper.

III

Jack disappeared shortly after his father's arrest on a charge of horse and cattle-stealing, and Tom, the prodigal, turned up unexpectedly. He was different from his father and eldest brother. He had an open good-humoured face, and was very kind-hearted; but was subject to peculiar fits of insanity, during which he did wild and foolish things for the mere love of notoriety. He had two natures—one bright and good, the other sullen and criminal. A taint of madness ran in the family—came down from drunken and unprincipled fathers of dead generations; under different conditions, it might have developed into genius in one or two—in Mary, perhaps.

"Cheer up, old woman!" cried Tom, patting his mother on the back. "We'll be happy yet. I've been wild and foolish, I know, and gave you some awful trouble, but that's all done with. I mean to keep steady, and by-and-bye we'll go away to Sydney or Queensland. Give us a smile, mother."

He got some "grubbing" to do, and for six months kept the family in provisions. Then a change came over him. He became moody and sullen—even brutal. He would sit for hours and grin to himself without any apparent cause; then he would stay away from home for days together.

"Tom's going wrong again," wailed Mrs. Wylie. "He'll get into trouble again, I know he will. We are disgraced enough already, God knows."

"You've done your best, mother," said Mary, "and can do no more. People will pity us; after all, the thing itself is not so bad as the everlasting dread of it. This will be a lesson for father—he wanted one—and maybe he'll be a better man." (She knew better than that.) "YOU did your best, mother."

"Ah, Mary! you don't know what I've gone through these thirty years in the bush with your father. I've had to go down on my knees and beg people not to prosecute him—and the same with your brother Tom; and this is the end of it."

"Better to have let them go, mother; you should have left father when you found out what sort of a man he was; it would have been better for all."

"It was my duty to stick by him, child; he was my husband. Your father was always a bad man, Mary—a bad man; I found it out too late. I could not tell you a quarter of what I have suffered with him.... I was proud, Mary; I wanted my children to be better than others.... It's my fault; it's a judgment.... I wanted to make my children better than others.... I was so proud, Mary."

Mary had a sweetheart, a drover, who was supposed to be in Queensland. He had promised to marry her, and take her and her mother away when he returned; at least, she had promised to marry him on that condition. He had now been absent on his latest trip for nearly six months, and there was no news from him. She got a copy of a country paper to look for the "stock passings"; but a startling headline caught her eye:

IMPUDENT ATTEMPT AT ROBBERY UNDER ARMS.—"A drover known to the police as Frederick Dunn, alias Drew, was arrested last week at—"

She read to the bitter end, and burned the paper. And the shadow of another trouble, darker and drearier than all the rest, was upon her.

So the little outcast family in Long Gully existed for several months, seeing no one save a sympathetic old splitter who would come and smoke his pipe by the fire of nights, and try to convince the old woman that matters might have been worse, and that she wouldn't worry so much if she knew the troubles of some of our biggest families, and that things would come out all right and the lesson would do Wylie good. Also, that Tom was a different boy altogether, and had more sense than to go wrong again. "It was nothing," he said, "nothing; they didn't know what trouble was."

But one day, when Mary and her mother were alone, the troopers came again.

"Mrs. Wylie, where's your son Tom?" they asked.

She sat still. She didn't even cry, "Oh, my God!"

"Don't be frightened, Mrs. Wylie," said one of the troopers, gently. "It ain't for much anyway, and maybe Tom'll be able to clear himself."

Mary sank on her knees by her mother's side, crying "Speak to me, mother. Oh, my God, she's dying! Speak for my sake, mother. Don't die, mother; it's all a mistake. Don't die and leave me here alone."

But the poor old woman was dead.

Wylie came out towards the end of the year, and a few weeks later he brought home a—another woman.

IV

Bob Bentley, general hawker, was camping under some rocks by the main road, near the foot of Long Gully. His mate was fast asleep under the tilted trap. Bob stood with his back to the fire, his pipe in his mouth, and his hands clasped behind him. The fire lit up the undersides of the branches above; a native bear sat in a fork blinking down at it, while the moon above him showed every hair on his ears. From among the trees came the pleasant jingle of hobble-chains, the slow tread of hoofs, and the "crunch, crunch" at the grass, as the horses moved about and grazed, now in moonlight, now in the soft shadows. "Old Thunder", a big black dog of no particular breed, gave a meaning look at his master, and started up the ridge, followed by several smaller dogs. Soon Bob heard from the hillside the "hy-yi-hi, whomp, whomp, whomp!" of old Thunder, and the yop-yop-yopping of the smaller fry—they had tree'd a 'possum. Bob threw himself on the grass, and pretended to be asleep. There was a sound as of a sizeable boulder rolling down the hill, and presently Thunder trotted round the fire to see if his master would come. Bob snored. The dog looked suspiciously at him, trotted round once or twice, and as a last resource gave him two great slobbery licks across the face. Bob got up with a good-natured oath.

"Well, old party," he said to Thunder, "you're a thundering old nuisance; but I s'pose you won't be satisfied till I come." He got a gun from the waggonette, loaded it, and started up the ridge; old Thunder rushing to and fro to show the way—as if the row the other dogs were making wasn't enough to guide his master.

When Bob returned with the 'possums he was startled to see a woman in the camp. She was sitting on a log by the fire, with her elbows on her knees and her face in her hands.

"Why—what the dev—who are you?"

The girl raised a white desperate face to him. It was Mary Wylie.

"My father and—and the woman—they're drinking—they turned me out! they turned me out."

"Did they now? I'm sorry for that. What can I do for you?... She's mad sure enough," he thought to himself; "I thought it was a ghost."

"I don't know," she wailed, "I don't know. You're a man, and I'm a helpless girl. They turned me out! My mother's dead, and my brothers gone away. Look! Look here!" pointing to a bruise on her forehead. "The woman did that. My own father stood by and saw it done—said it served me right! Oh, my God!"

"What woman? Tell me all about it."

"The woman father brought home!... I want to go away from the bush! Oh! for God's sake take me away from the bush!... Anything! anything!—you know!—only take me away from the bush!"

Bob and his mate—who had been roused—did their best to soothe her; but suddenly, without a moment's warning, she sprang to her feet and scrambled to the top of the rock overhanging the camp. She stood for a moment in the bright moonlight, gazing intently down the vacant road.

"Here they come!" she cried, pointing down the road. "Here they come—the troopers! I can see their cap-peaks glistening in the moonlight!... I'm going away! Mother's gone. I'm going now!—Good-bye!—Good-bye! I'm going away from the bush!"

Then she ran through the trees towards the foot of Long Gully. Bob and his mate followed; but, being unacquainted with the locality, they lost her.

She ran to the edge of a granite cliff on the higher side of the deepest of the rocky waterholes. There was a heavy splash, and three startled kangaroos, who had been drinking, leapt back and sped away, like three grey ghosts, up the ridge towards the moonlit peak.

Mitchell on the "Sex" and Other "Problems"

"I agree with 'T' in last week's 'Bulletin'," said Mitchell, after cogitating some time over the last drop of tea in his pannikin, held at various angles, "about what they call the 'Sex Problem'. There's no problem, really, except Creation, and that's not our affair; we can't solve it, and we've no right to make a problem out of it for ourselves to puzzle over, and waste the little time that is given us about. It's we that make the problems, not Creation. We make 'em, and they only smother us; they'll smother the world in the end if we don't look out. Anything that can be argued, for and against, from half a dozen different points of view—and most things that men argue over can be—and anything that has been argued about for thousands of years (as most things have) is worse than profitless; it wastes the world's time and ours, and often wrecks old mateships. Seems to me the deeper you read, think, talk, or write about things that end in ism, the less satisfactory the result; the more likely you are to get bushed and dissatisfied with the world. And the more you keep on the surface of plain things, the plainer the sailing—the more comfortable for you and everybody else. We've always got to come to the surface to breathe, in the end, in any case; we're meant to live on the surface, and we might as well stay there and look after it and ourselves for all the good we do diving down after fish that aren't there, except in our imagination. And some of 'em are very dead fish, too—the 'Sex Problem', for instance. When we fall off the surface of the earth it will be time enough to make a problem out of the fact that we couldn't stick on. I'm a Federal Pro-trader in this country; I'm a Federalist because I think Federation is the plain and natural course for Australia, and I'm a Free-tectionist because I'm in favour of sinking any question, or any two things, that enlightened people can argue and fight over, and try, one after the other, for fifty years without being able to come to a decision about, or prove which is best for the welfare of the country. It only wastes a young country's time, and keeps it off the right track. Federation isn't a problem—it's a plain fact—but they make a problem out of every panel they have to push down in the rotten old boundary fences."

"Personal interests," suggested Joe.

"Of course. It's personal interest of the wrong sort that makes all the problems. You can trace the sex problem to people who trade in unhealthy personal interests. I believe in personal interests of the right sort—true individualism. If we all looked after ourselves, and our wives and families—if we have any—in the proper way, the world would be all right. We waste too much time looking after each other.

"Now, supposing we're travelling and have to get a shed and make a cheque so's to be able to send a few quid home, as soon as we can, to the missus, or the old folks, and the next water is twenty miles ahead. If we sat down and argued over a social problem till doomsday, we wouldn't get to the tank; we'd die of thirst, and the missus and kids, or the old folks, would be sold up and turned out into the streets, and have to fall back on a 'home of hope', or wait their turn at the Benevolent Asylum with bags for broken victuals. I've seen that, and I don't want anybody belonging to me to have to do it.

"Reminds me that when a poor, deserted girl goes to a 'home' they don't make a problem of her—they do their best for her and try to get her righted. And the priests, too: if there's anything in the sex or any other problem—anything that hasn't been threshed out—they're the men that'll know it. I'm not a Catholic, but I know this: that if a girl that's been left by one—no matter what Church she belongs to—goes to the priest, they'll work all the points they know (and they know 'em all) to get her righted, and, if the chap, or his people, won't come up to the scratch, Father Ryan'll frighten hell out of 'em. I can't say as much for our own Churches."

"But you're in favour of socialism and democracy?" asked Joe.

"Of course I am. But the world won't do any good arguing over it. The people will have to get up and walk, and, what's more, stick together—and I don't think they'll ever do that—it ain't in human nature. Socialism, or democracy, was all right in this country till it got fashionable and was made a fad or a problem of. Then it got smothered pretty quick. And a fad or a problem always breeds a host of parasites or hangers-on. Why, as soon as I saw the advanced idealist fools—they're generally the middle-class, shabby-genteel families that catch Spiritualism and Theosophy and those sort of complaints, at the end of the epidemic—that catch on at the tail-end of things and think they've caught something brand, shining, new;—as soon as I saw them, and the problem spielers and notoriety-hunters of both sexes, beginning to hang round Australian Unionism, I knew it was doomed. And so it was. The straight men were disgusted, or driven out. There are women who hang on for the same reason that a girl will sometimes go into the dock and swear an innocent man's life away. But as soon as they see that the cause is dying, they drop it at once, and wait for another. They come like bloody dingoes round a calf, and only leave the bones. They're about as democratic as the crows. And the rotten 'sex-problem' sort of thing is the cause of it all; it poisons weak minds—and strong ones too sometimes.

"Why, you could make a problem out of Epsom salts. You might argue as to why human beings want Epsom salts, and try to trace the causes that led up to it. I don't like the taste of Epsom salts—it's nasty in the mouth—but when I feel that way I take 'em, and I feel better afterwards; and that's good enough for me. We might argue that black is white, and white is black, and neither of 'em is anything, and nothing is everything; and a woman's a man and a man's a woman, and it's really the man that has the youngsters, only we imagine it's the woman because she imagines that she has all the pain and trouble, and the doctor is under the impression that he's attending to her, not the man, and the man thinks so too because he imagines he's walking up and down outside, and slipping into the corner pub now and then for a nip to keep his courage up, waiting, when it's his wife that's doing that all the time; we might argue that it's all force of imagination, and that imagination is an unknown force, and that the unknown is nothing. But, when we've settled all that to our own satisfaction, how much further ahead are we? In the end we'll come to the conclusion that we ain't alive, and never existed, and then we'll leave off bothering, and the world will go on just the same."

"What about science?" asked Joe.

"Science ain't 'sex problems'; it's facts.... Now, I don't mind Spiritualism and those sort of things; they might help to break the monotony, and can't do much harm. But the 'sex problem', as it's written about to-day, does; it's dangerous and dirty, and it's time to settle it with a club. Science and education, if left alone, will look after sex facts.

"You can't get anything out of the 'sex problem', no matter how you argue. In the old Bible times they had half a dozen wives each, but we don't know for certain how THEY got on. The Mormons tried it again, and seemed to get on all right till we interfered. We don't seem to be able to get on with one wife now—at least, according to the 'sex problem'. The 'sex problem' troubled the Turks so much that they tried three. Lots of us try to settle it by knocking round promiscuously, and that leads to actions for maintenance and breach of promise cases, and all sorts of trouble. Our blacks settle the 'sex problem' with a club, and so far I haven't heard any complaints from them.

"Take hereditary causes and surrounding circumstances, for instance. In order to understand or judge a man right, you would need to live under the same roof with him from childhood, and under the same roofs, or tents, with his parents, right back to Adam, and then you'd be blocked for want of more ancestors through which to trace the causes that led to Abel—I mean Cain—going on as he did. What's the use or sense of it? You might argue away in any direction for a million miles and a million years back into the past, but you've got to come back to where you are if you wish to do any good for yourself, or anyone else.

"Sometimes it takes you a long while to get back to where you are—sometimes you never do it. Why, when those controversies were started in the 'Bulletin' about the kangaroos and other things, I thought I knew something about the bush. Now I'm damned if I'm sure I could tell a kangaroo from a wombat.

"Trying to find out things is the cause of all the work and trouble in this world. It was Eve's fault in the first place—or Adam's, rather, because it might be argued that he should have been master. Some men are too lazy to be masters in their own homes, and run the show properly; some are too careless, and some too drunk most of their time, and some too weak. If Adam and Eve hadn't tried to find out things there'd have been no toil and trouble in the world to-day; there'd have been no bloated capitalists, and no horny-handed working men, and no politics, no freetrade and protection—and no clothes. The woman next door wouldn't be able to pick holes in your wife's washing on the line. We'd have been all running about in a big Garden of Eden with nothing on, and nothing to do except loaf, and make love, and lark, and laugh, and play practical jokes on each other."

Joe grinned.

"That would have been glorious. Wouldn't it, Joe? There'd have been no 'sex problem' then."

William Spencer stayed away from school that hot day, and "went swimming". The master wrote a note to William's father, and gave it to William's brother Joe to carry home.

"You'll give that to your father to-night, Joseph."

"Yes, sir."

Bill waited for Joe near the gap, and walked home with him.

"I s'pose you've got a note for father."

"Yes," said Joe.

"I s'pose you know what's in it?"

"Ye—yes. Oh, why did you stop away, Bill?"

"You don't mean to say that you're dirty mean enough to give it to father? Hey?"

"I must, Will. I promised the master."

"He needn't never know."

"Oh, yes, he will. He's coming over to our place on Saturday, and he's sure to ask me to-morrow."

Pause.

"Look here, Joe!" said Bill, "I don't want to get a hiding and go without supper to-night. I promised to go 'possuming with Johnny Nowlett, and he's going to give me a fire out of his gun. You can come, too. I don't want to cop out on it to-night—if I do I'll run away from home again, so there."

Bill walked on a bit in moody, Joe in troubled, silence.

Bill tried again: he threatened, argued, and pleaded, but Joe was firm. "The master trusted me, Will," he said.

"Joe," said Bill at last, after a long pause, "I wouldn't do it to you."

Joe was troubled.

"I wouldn't do it to you, Joe."

Joe thought how Bill had stood up and fought for him only last week.

"I'd tear the note in bits; I'd tell a hundred lies; I'd take a dozen hidings first, Joe—I would."

Joe was greatly troubled. His chest heaved, and the tears came to his eyes.

"I'd do more than that for you, Joe, and you know it."

Joe knew it. They were crossing the old goldfield now. There was a shaft close to the path; it had fallen in, funnel-shaped, at the top, but was still thirty or forty feet deep; some old logs were jammed across about five feet down. Joe suddenly snatched the note from his pocket and threw it in. It fluttered to the other side and rested on a piece of the old timber. Bill saw it, but said nothing, and, seeing their father coming home from work, they hurried on.

Joe was deep in trouble now. Bill tried to comfort and cheer him, but it was no use. Bill promised never to run away from home any more, to go to school every day, and never to fight, or steal, or tell lies. But Joe had betrayed his trust for the first time in his life, and wouldn't be comforted.

Some time in the night Bill woke, and found Joe sitting up in bed crying.

"Why, what's the matter, Joe?"

"I never done a mean thing like that before," sobbed Joe. "I wished I'd chucked meself down the shaft instead. The master trusted me, Will; an' now, if he asks me to-morrow, I'll have to tell a lie."

"Then tell the truth, Joe, an' take the hidin'; it'll soon be over—just a couple of cuts with the cane and it'll be all over."

"Oh, no, it won't. He won't never trust me any more. I've never been caned in that school yet, Will, and if I am I'll never go again. Oh! why will you run away from home, Will, and play the wag, and steal, and get us all into such trouble? You don't know how mother takes on about it—you don't know how it hurts father! I've deceived the master, and mother and father to-day, just because you're so—so selfish," and he laid down and cried himself to sleep.

Bill lay awake and thought till daylight; then he got up quietly, put on his clothes, and stole away from the house and across the flat, followed by the dog, who thought it was a 'possum-hunting expedition. Bill wished the dog would not be quite so demonstrative, at least until they got away from the house. He went straight to the shaft, let himself down carefully on to one of the old logs, and stooped to pick up the note, gleaming white in the sickly summer daylight. Then the rotten timber gave way suddenly, without a moment's warning.

They found him that morning at about nine o'clock. The dog attracted the attention of an old fossicker passing to his work. The letter was gripped in Bill's right hand when they brought him up. They took him home, and the father went for a doctor. Bill came to himself a little just before the last, and said: "Mother! I wasn't running away, mother—tell father that—I—I wanted to try and catch a 'possum on the ground.... Where's Joe? I want Joe. Go out, mother, a minute, and send Joe."

"Here I am, Bill," said Joe, in a choking, terrified voice.

"Has the master been yet?"

"No."

"Bend down, Joe. I went for the note, and the logs gave way. I meant to be back before they was up. I dropped it down inside the bed; you watch your chance and get it; and say you forgot it last night—say you didn't like to give it—that won't be a lie. Tell the master I'm—I'm sorry—tell the master never to send no notes no more—except by girls—that's all.... Mother! Take the blankets off me—I'm dyin'."

The Story of the Oracle

"We young fellows," said "Sympathy Joe" to Mitchell, after tea, in their first camp west the river—"and you and I ARE young fellows, comparatively—think we know the world. There are plenty of young chaps knocking round in this country who reckon they've been through it all before they're thirty. I've met cynics and men-o'-the-world, aged twenty-one or thereabouts, who've never been further than a trip to Sydney. They talk about 'this world' as if they'd knocked around in half-a-dozen other worlds before they came across here—and they are just as off-hand about it as older Australians are when they talk about this colony as compared with the others. They say: 'My oath!—same here.' 'I've been there.' 'My oath!—you're right.' 'Take it from me!' and all that sort of thing. They understand women, and have a contempt for 'em; and chaps that don't talk as they talk, or do as they do, or see as they see, are either soft or ratty. A good many reckon that 'life ain't blanky well worth livin''; sometimes they feel so blanky somehow that they wouldn't give a blank whether they chucked it or not; but that sort never chuck it. It's mostly the quiet men that do that, and if they've got any complaints to make against the world they make 'em at the head station. Why, I've known healthy, single, young fellows under twenty-five who drank to drown their troubles—some because they reckoned the world didn't understand nor appreciate 'em—as if it COULD!"

"If the world don't understand or appreciate you," said Mitchell solemnly, as he reached for a burning stick to light his pipe—"MAKE it!"

"To drown THEIR troubles!" continued Joe, in a tone of impatient contempt. "The Oracle must be well on towards the sixties; he can take his glass with any man, but you never saw him drunk."

"What's the Oracle to do with it?"

"Did you ever hear his history?"

"No. Do you know it?"

"Yes, though I don't think he has any idea that I do. Now, we were talking about the Oracle a little while ago. We know he's an old ass; a good many outsiders consider that he's a bit soft or ratty, and, as we're likely to be mates together for some time on that fencing contract, if we get it, you might as well know what sort of a man he is and was, so's you won't get uneasy about him if he gets deaf for a while when you're talking, or does funny things with his pipe or pint-pot, or walks up and down by himself for an hour or so after tea, or sits on a log with his head in his hands, or leans on the fence in the gloaming and keeps looking in a blank sort of way, straight ahead, across the clearing. For he's gazing at something a thousand miles across country, south-east, and about twenty years back into the past, and no doubt he sees himself (as a young man), and a Gippsland girl, spooning under the stars along between the hop-gardens and the Mitchell River. And, if you get holt of a fiddle or a concertina, don't rasp or swank too much on old tunes, when he's round, for the Oracle can't stand it. Play something lively. He'll be down there at that surveyor's camp yarning till all hours, so we'll have plenty of time for the story—but don't you ever give him a hint that you know.

"My people knew him well; I got most of the story from them—mostly from Uncle Bob, who knew him better than any. The rest leaked out through the women—you know how things leak out amongst women?"

Mitchell dropped his head and scratched the back of it. HE knew.

"It was on the Cudgegong River. My Uncle Bob was mates with him on one of those 'rushes' along there—the 'Pipeclay', I think it was, or the 'Log Paddock'. The Oracle was a young man then, of course, and so was Uncle Bob (he was a match for most men). You see the Oracle now, and you can imagine what he was when he was a young man. Over six feet, and as straight as a sapling, Uncle Bob said, clean-limbed, and as fresh as they made men in those days; carried his hands behind him, as he does now, when he hasn't got the swag—but his shoulders were back in those days. Of course he wasn't the Oracle then; he was young Tom Marshall—but that doesn't matter. Everybody liked him—especially women and children. He was a bit happy-go-lucky and careless, but he didn't know anything about 'this world', and didn't bother about it; he hadn't 'been there'. 'And his heart was as good as gold,' my aunt used to say. He didn't understand women as we young fellows do nowadays, and therefore he hadn't any contempt for 'em. Perhaps he understood, and understands, them better than any of us, without knowing it. Anyway, you know, he's always gentle and kind where a woman or child is concerned, and doesn't like to hear us talk about women as we do sometimes.

"There was a girl on the goldfields—a fine lump of a blonde, and pretty gay. She came from Sydney, I think, with her people, who kept shanties on the fields. She had a splendid voice, and used to sing 'Madeline'. There might have been one or two bad women before that, in the Oracle's world, but no cold-blooded, designing ones. He calls the bad ones 'unfortunate'.

"Perhaps it was Tom's looks, or his freshness, or his innocence, or softness—or all together—that attracted her. Anyway, he got mixed up with her before the goldfield petered out.

"No doubt it took a long while for the facts to work into Tom's head that a girl might sing like she did and yet be thoroughly unprincipled. The Oracle was always slow at coming to a decision, but when he does it's generally the right one. Anyway, you can take that for granted, for you won't move him.

"I don't know whether he found out that she wasn't all that she pretended to be to him, or whether they quarrelled, or whether she chucked him over for a lucky digger. Tom never had any luck on the goldfields. Anyway, he left and went over to the Victorian side, where his people were, and went up Gippsland way. It was there for the first time in his life that he got what you would call 'properly gone on a girl'; he got hard hit—he met his fate.

"Her name was Bertha Bredt, I remember. Aunt Bob saw her afterwards. Aunt Bob used to say that she was 'a girl as God made her'—a good, true, womanly girl—one of those sort of girls that only love once. Tom got on with her father, who was packing horses through the ranges to the new goldfields—it was rough country and there were no roads; they had to pack everything there in those days, and there was money in it. The girl's father took to Tom—as almost everybody else did—and, as far as the girl was concerned, I think it was a case of love at first sight. They only knew each other for about six months, and were only 'courting' (as they called it then) for three or four months altogether, but she was that sort of girl that can love a man for six weeks and lose him for ever, and yet go on loving him to the end of her life—and die with his name on her lips.

"Well, things were brightening up every way for Tom, and he and his sweetheart were beginning to talk about their own little home in future, when there came a letter from the 'Madeline' girl in New South Wales.

"She was in terrible trouble. Her baby was to be born in a month. Her people had kicked her out, and she was in danger of starving. She begged and prayed of him to come back and marry her, if only for his child's sake. He could go then, and be free; she would never trouble him any more—only come and marry her for the child's sake.

"The Oracle doesn't know where he lost that letter, but I do. It was burnt afterwards by a woman, who was more than a mother to him in his trouble—Aunt Bob. She thought he might carry it round with the rest of his papers, in his swag, for years, and come across it unexpectedly when he was camped by himself in the bush and feeling dull. It wouldn't have done him any good then.

"He must have fought the hardest fight in his life when he got that letter. No doubt he walked to and fro, to and fro, all night, with his hands behind him, and his eyes on the ground, as he does now sometimes. Walking up and down helps you to fight a thing out.

"No doubt he thought of things pretty well as he thinks now: the poor girl's shame on every tongue, and belled round the district by every hag in the township; and she looked upon by women as being as bad as any man who ever went to Bathurst in the old days, handcuffed between two troopers. There is sympathy, a pipe and tobacco, a cheering word, and, maybe, a whisky now and then, for the criminal on his journey; but there is no mercy, at least as far as women are concerned, for the poor foolish girl, who has to sneak out the back way and round by back streets and lanes after dark, with a cloak on to hide her figure.

"Tom sent what money he thought he could spare, and next day he went to the girl he loved and who loved him, and told her the truth, and showed her the letter. She was only a girl—but the sort of girl you COULD go to in a crisis like that. He had made up his mind to do the right thing, and she loved him all the more for it. And so they parted.

"When Tom reached 'Pipeclay', the girl's relations, that she was stopping with, had a parson readied up, and they were married the same day."

"And what happened after that?" asked Mitchell.

"Nothing happened for three or four months; then the child was born. It wasn't his!"

Mitchell stood up with an oath.

"The girl was thoroughly bad. She'd been carrying on with God knows how many men, both before and after she trapped Tom."

"And what did he do then?"

"Well, you know how the Oracle argues over things, and I suppose he was as big an old fool then as he is now. He thinks that, as most men would deceive women if they could, when one man gets caught, he's got no call to squeal about it; he's bound, because of the sins of men in general against women, to make the best of it. What is one man's wrong counted against the wrongs of hundreds of unfortunate girls.

"It's an uncommon way of arguing—like most of the Oracle's ideas—but it seems to look all right at first sight.

"Perhaps he thought she'd go straight; perhaps she convinced him that he was the cause of her first fall; anyway he stuck to her for more than a year, and intended to take her away from that place as soon as he'd scraped enough money together. It might have gone on up till now, if the father of the child—a big black Irishman named Redmond—hadn't come sneaking back at the end of a year. He—well, he came hanging round Mrs. Marshall while Tom was away at work—and she encouraged him. And Tom was forced to see it.

"Tom wanted to fight out his own battle without interference, but the chaps wouldn't let him—they reckoned that he'd stand very little show against Redmond, who was a very rough customer and a fighting man. My uncle Bob, who was there still, fixed it up this way: The Oracle was to fight Redmond, and if the Oracle got licked Uncle Bob was to take Redmond on. If Redmond whipped Uncle Bob, that was to settle it; but if Uncle Bob thrashed Redmond, then he was also to fight Redmond's mate, another big, rough Paddy named Duigan. Then the affair would be finished—no matter which way the last bout went. You see, Uncle Bob was reckoned more of a match for Redmond than the Oracle was, so the thing looked fair enough—at first sight.

"Redmond had his mate, Duigan, and one or two others of the rough gang that used to terrorise the fields round there in the roaring days of Gulgong. The Oracle had Uncle Bob, of course, and long Dave Regan, the drover—a good-hearted, sawny kind of chap that'd break the devil's own buck-jumper, or smash him, or get smashed himself—and little Jimmy Nowlett, the bullocky, and one or two of the old, better-class diggers that were left on the field.

"There's a clear space among the saplings in Specimen Gully, where they used to pitch circuses; and here, in the cool of a summer evening, the two men stood face to face. Redmond was a rough, roaring, foul-mouthed man; he stripped to his shirt, and roared like a bull, and swore, and sneered, and wanted to take the whole of Tom's crowd while he was at it, and make one clean job of 'em. Couldn't waste time fighting them all one after the other, because he wanted to get away to the new rush at Cattle Creek next day. The fool had been drinking shanty-whisky.

"Tom stood up in his clean, white moles and white flannel shirt—one of those sort with no sleeves, that give the arms play. He had a sort of set expression and a look in his eyes that Uncle Bob—nor none of them—had ever seen there before. 'Give us plenty of—room!' roared Redmond; 'one of us is going to hell, now! This is going to be a fight to a—finish, and a—short one!' And it was!" Joe paused.

"Go on," said Mitchell—"go on!"

Joe drew a long breath.

"The Oracle never got a mark! He was top-dog right from the start. Perhaps it was his strength that Redmond had underrated, or his want of science that puzzled him, or the awful silence of the man that frightened him (it made even Uncle Bob uneasy). Or, perhaps, it was Providence (it was a glorious chance for Providence), but, anyway, as I say, the Oracle never got a mark, except on his knuckles. After a few rounds Redmond funked and wanted to give in, but the chaps wouldn't let him—not even his own mates—except Duigan. They made him take it as long as he could stand on his feet. He even shammed to be knocked out, and roared out something about having broken his—ankle—but it was no use. And the Oracle! The chaps that knew thought that he'd refuse to fight, and never hit a man that had given in. But he did. He just stood there with that quiet look in his eyes and waited, and, when he did hit, there wasn't any necessity for Redmond to PRETEND to be knocked down. You'll see a glint of that old light in the Oracle's eyes even now, once in a while; and when you do it's a sign that you or someone are going too far, and had better pull up, for it's a red light on the line, old as he is.

"Now, Jimmy Nowlett was a nuggety little fellow, hard as cast iron, good-hearted, but very excitable; and when the bashed Redmond was being carted off (poor Uncle Bob was always pretty high-strung, and was sitting on a log sobbing like a great child from the reaction), Duigan made some sneering remark that only Jimmy Nowlett caught, and in an instant he was up and at Duigan.

"Perhaps Duigan was demoralised by his mate's defeat, or by the suddenness of the attack; but, at all events, he got a hiding, too. Uncle Bob used to say that it was the funniest thing he ever saw in his life. Jimmy kept yelling: 'Let me get at him! By the Lord, let me get at him!' And nobody was attempting to stop him, he WAS getting at him all the time—and properly, too; and, when he'd knocked Duigan down, he'd dance round him and call on him to get up; and every time he jumped or bounced, he'd squeak like an india-rubber ball, Uncle Bob said, and he would nearly burst his boiler trying to lug the big man on to his feet so's he could knock him down again. It took two of Jimmy's mates all their time to lam him down into a comparatively reasonable state of mind after the fight was over.

"The Oracle left for Sydney next day, and Uncle Bob went with him. He stayed at Uncle Bob's place for some time. He got very quiet, they said, and gentle; he used to play with the children, and they got mighty fond of him. The old folks thought his heart was broken, but it went through a deeper sorrow still after that and it ain't broken yet. It takes a lot to break the heart of a man."

"And his wife," asked Mitchell—"what became of her?"

"I don't think he ever saw her again. She dropped down pretty low after he left her—I've heard she's living somewhere quietly. The Oracle's been sending someone money ever since I knew him, and I know it's a woman. I suppose it's she. He isn't the sort of a man to see a woman starve—especially a woman he had ever had anything to do with."

"And the Gippsland girl?" asked Mitchell.

"That's the worst part of it all, I think. The Oracle went up North somewhere. In the course of a year or two his affair got over Gippsland way through a mate of his who lived over there, and at last the story got to the ears of this girl, Bertha Bredt. She must have written a dozen letters to him, Aunt Bob said. She knew what was in 'em, but, of course, she'd never tell us. The Oracle only wrote one in reply. Then, what must the girl do but clear out from home and make her way over to Sydney—to Aunt Bob's place, looking for Tom. She never got any further. She took ill—brain-fever, or broken heart, or something of that sort. All the time she was down her cry was—'I want to see him! I want to find Tom! I only want to see Tom!'

"When they saw she was dying, Aunt Bob wired to the Oracle to come—and he came. When the girl saw it was Tom sitting by the bed, she just gave one long look in his face, put her arms round his neck, and laid her head on his shoulder—and died.... Here comes the Oracle now."

Mitchell lifted the tea-billy on to the coals.

Henry Archibald Hertzberg Lawson was born on the 17th June 1867 in a town on the Grenfell goldfields of New South Wales, Australia.

His parents, father Niel, a Norwegian born miner and mother Louisa, a noted poet, publisher and feminist were married on 7th July 1866 when he was 32 and she 18. On Henry's birth, the family surname was Anglicised to Lawson. The couple were to have an unhappy marriage despite producing three children.

Lawson attended school at Eurunderee from October 1876 but an ear infection he contracted left him partially deaf. By fourteen he had lost his hearing completely.

Lawson later attended a Catholic school at Mudgee, New South Wales where he developed an interest in poetry and, on his mother's influence, immersed himself in books given that learning in the classroom, with his deafness, was a major hurdle.

In 1883, after working on construction jobs with his father in the Blue Mountains, Lawson joined his mother in Sydney where she was living with his siblings. Here, Lawson worked during the day and studied at night for his matriculation in the hopes of enrolling at university. However, he failed his exams.

His first published poem was 'A Song of the Republic' in The Bulletin on 1st October 1887. This was quickly followed by other published poems with one recognising him as "a youth whose poetic genius here speaks eloquently for itself."

In 1890 he began a relationship with Mary Gilmore but it broke down due to his frequent absences from Sydney.

Lawson received an offer to write for the Brisbane Boomerang in 1891, but financial troubles at the magazine made this a short stint of only a few months. Despite writing for other magazines in Brisbane it was a dead end.

He returned to Sydney and continued to write for the Bulletin which, in 1892, engaged him for an inland trip where he could write articles about the harsh realities of life in drought-stricken New South Wales. He also took some time to work as a roustabout (an unskilled or semi-skilled worker) in the woolshed at Toorale Station. This resulted in his contributions to the Bulletin Debate and became the experience he used for a number of his stories in subsequent years. For Lawson this was an eye-opening period. His grim view of the outback was far removed from the romantic idyll of bravery and beauty inked in the poetry of his contemporary Banjo Paterson.

In 1896, Lawson married Bertha Bredt, Jr., daughter of Bertha Bredt, the prominent socialist. The marriage ended very unhappily in June 1903. They had two children.

Despite this Lawson was finding his way in the literary world. His writing was achieving recognition. His most successful prose collection 'While the Billy Boils', was published in 1896. In it he virtually reinvented Australian realism.

His writing style of short, sharp sentences with honed and sparse descriptions created a personal writing style that defined Australians: dryly laconic, passionately egalitarian and deeply humane. Most of Lawson's work centres on the Australian bush, it's fabled outback, such as in the desolate 'Past Carin', and is considered by many to vividly portray the real Australian life at that time.

Like the majority of Australians, Lawson lived in a city, but had had plenty of experience in outback life, these two outlooks helped shape a very individual talent. Unfortunately, his life was also flawed with other issues.

In Sydney in 1898 he was a prominent member of the Dawn and Dusk Club, a bohemian club of writer friends who met for drinks and conversation.

Sadly, for Lawson despite his growing recognition and fame he became withdrawn and unable to take part in the usual routines of life. His struggles with alcohol and mental health issues continued to drain him. His once prolific literary output began to decline. At times he was destitute mainly due, despite good sales and an enthusiastic audience, to ruinous publishing deals he had entered into.

In 1903 he bought a room at Mrs Isabel Byers' Coffee Palace in North Sydney. This near 20-year friendship between Mrs Byers and Lawson was a bedrock for him. Despite his position as the most celebrated Australian writer of the time, Lawson was deeply depressed and perpetually poor. His ex-wife repeatedly reported him for non-payment of child maintenance, which resulted in numerous jail terms or periods in psychiatric institutions. He was incarcerated at Darlinghurst Gaol for drunkenness, wife desertion, child desertion, and non-payment of child support seven times between 1905 and 1909 and spent a total of 159 days in prison. He wrote about these experiences in the haunting poem 'One Hundred and Three'—his prison number—which was published in 1908.

Mrs Byers was a good poet herself and, although of modest education, had been writing vivid poetry since her teens in a somewhat similar style to Lawson's. Long separated from her husband and elderly, Mrs Byers was, at the time she met Lawson, a woman of independent means looking forward to a comfortable retirement. She regarded Lawson as Australia's greatest living poet, and hoped to sustain him well enough to keep him writing. She acted as his agent in negotiations with publishers, helped to arrange contact with his children, contacted friends and supporters to help him financially, as well as assisting and nursing him through his mental health issues and problems with alcohol. She wrote countless letters on his behalf and pursued any avenue that could provide Lawson with financial support or a publishing deal.

Regardless of all else Lawson was a vocal nationalist and republican and took pride that many of his works were helping to establish the Australian vernacular in fiction.

Henry Archibald Hertzberg Lawson died, of a cerebral hemorrhage, in Mrs Byer's home in Abbotsford, Sydney on 2nd September 1922.

Lawson became the first Australian writer to be granted a state funeral. It was attended by the Prime Minister Billy Hughes and the (later) Premier of New South Wales, Jack Lang (the husband of Lawson's sister-in-law Hilda Bredt), as well as thousands of citizens.

Henry Lawson – A Concise Bibliography

Short Stories in Prose and Verse (1894)
While the Billy Boils (1896)
In the Days When the World was Wide and Other Verses (1896)
Verses, Popular and Humorous (1900)
On the Track (1900)
Over the Sliprails (1900)
On the Track, and, Over the Sliprails (1900)
Popular Verses (1900)
Humorous Verses (1900)
The Country I Come From (1901)
Joe Wilson and His Mates (1901)
Children of the Bush (1902)
When I Was King and Other Verses (1905)
The Elder Son (1905)
When I Was King (1905)
The Romance of the Swag (1907)
Send Round the Hat (1907)
The Skyline Riders and Other Verses (1910)
The Rising of the Court and Other Sketches in Prose and Verse (1910)
For Australia and Other Poems (1913)
Triangles of Life and Other Stories (1913)
My Army, O, My Army! and Other Songs (1915)
Song of the Dardanelles and Other Verses (1916)
Selected Poems of Henry Lawson (1918)